GATEWAY TO THE PAST

******

SECRETS OF THE BIRD CAGE THEATER

MANUELA SCHNEIDER

WOLFPACK
PUBLISHING
— EST 2013 —

WOLFPACK
PUBLISHING
— EST 2013 —

GATEWAY TO THE PAST

******

SECRETS OF THE BIRD CAGE THEATER

ACKNOWLEDGEMENTS

***

CHERYL LEAVERE HONEYCUTT

Cheryl inspired me with her outgoing, ambitious personality to create the character of Cheryl Roberts in this book. Cheryl is a true power lady and a modern-day pioneer.

I want to thank the following people for making this book possible:

My wonderful editor Denise F. Mc Allister. Not only has she done a fabulous job editing my books but also blessed me with great advice and expertise.

My publicist Krista Rolfzen Soukup and her firm Blue Cottage Agency designed a new path for me to follow my dream.

Best-selling author Harlan Hague, who has helped me tremendously on my way to self-publishing.

CHAPTER 1

***

LISA STEPPED OUT OF THE DOOR ONTO THE WEATHERED BOARDWALK. THE TOWN was quiet and Allen Street empty. She lit a cigarette with the Zippo lighter her boyfriend had given her for her last birthday and smiled as she returned it to her red purse.

The tired woman remained in front of the saloon, smoking for a minute or two, trying to unwind from her waitressing shift. Turning right, she slowly walked beside the closed shops and bars toward the parking lot behind the small hill at the upper part of Allen Street. Her boot heels produced a hollow sound on the wooden planks of the boardwalk. It was a normal weekday, and the saloon had closed early due to the lack of paying guests. There hadn't been any live music today either. Big Nose Kate's was one of the best-known hangouts in the entire Southwest, but the place definitely hadn't been busy lately.

As a matter of fact, the entire town was kind of deserted these days. The shop owners complained on a daily basis about the unsatisfying number of tourists during the past few months.

And, as usual, people blamed everyone else for the

weak economy and the town's lousy business development. Tombstone was not different from other places when it came to politics.

Tombstone depended on its visitors and their precious dollars. One thing was sure, the guests from all over the country had become stingy lately, not wanting to spend much cash in town, at least not like in the old days. Folks didn't want to pay admission to shows and museums and didn't buy much in the stores either. But even worse was the fact that the number of tourists was dropping steadily. So far, the town's mayor still emphasized the fact that Tombstone drew 1.5 million visitors each year but it surely didn't feel like so many of them dropped in lately. Lisa and other townsfolk had doubted that number quite often in public.

"Well, can't change the situation today so I'd better hit the road," she mumbled, puffing on her cigarette while walking toward her car. Lisa's work colleagues knew well that she hated boring evening shifts with a small number of guests. What aggravated her even more were the lousy tips that resulted. Tonight, her shift had been never-ending, dragging for most members of the crew with the usual townsfolk around them. She hadn't even paid attention to what the people had talked about at the bar.

The pretty waitress stopped in her tracks and pulled on her cigarette one last time, leaving blood-red lipstick marks on the butt. Small sparks glinted on the tip as she tossed it into the dirt-covered street.

She hadn't been aware that she stood right in front of the Bird Cage Theatre with its dark windows staring back. A sudden cold breeze touched her cheek and she shivered. Lisa cautiously looked back at the façade of the building. She told her boyfriend that she had never liked the Bird

Cage. In her opinion, it was the eeriest spot in town.

There was something about the building which didn't seem right to her. Lisa knew it was one of the few original buildings from Tombstone's heyday that had survived the big fires of 1881 and 1882. But even her boyfriend couldn't convince her to pay a visit to the museum inside.

Since she wanted to get home as fast as possible, Lisa turned on her heel and hurried past the dark building toward her car. She never shook off the chill even as she drove toward Sierra Vista where she lived and kept the car's heater on full blast all the way to the parking lot of her apartment complex.

Later, Allen Street, 1:45 a.m. No one was out on the road, not even a stray cat or dog. The weather was calm, the night, dark with a slight trace of silvery moonlight behind a few puffy clouds. The town slept. The former theater lay in complete darkness. If anyone had been walking along the boardwalk, they would have heard the soft clinking of glasses as toasts were made, accompanied by the high-pitched giggles of fallen angels from days long gone.

Maybe someone would have heard the muted sound of the old-fashioned piano drifting through the doors onto the empty street. But no one was outside at this late hour and so the old building kept living its own life of a long-forgotten time in the middle of the night.

CHAPTER 2

***

CHERYL WAS ANGRY AND CURSED LOUDLY. OF ALL THE PLACES SHE HAD applied, it had to be this god-forsaken Western town that sent her news of her appointment with the Arizona State Parks organization.

Studying tourism management included a trainee placement at a tourist site of interest. Her application had been accepted by the Arizona State Parks. At first, she had been thrilled about it but instead of being signed up as a ranger to one of the major spots such as the Red Rock State Park or Lake Havasu, as she had hoped, she had been assigned to the Courthouse Museum in dusty Tombstone. That was literally in the middle of nowhere. God, all she had ever heard about Tombstone was that the town reeked with Western history, and Hollywood had made some movies about Tombstone. End of story.

To hell with reenacting wannabe Earps. She wanted to be in a spot that easily drew 20,000 people a day from all over the world. The busier, the better. After all, she was a real city girl. But according to the Arizona State Parks management, all other job openings were filled by the time they had decided to hire her, so Cheryl had no choice but to try to make the best of the situation. After all, it was only for four months, five at the most. The time would pass quickly, she tried to reassure herself.

So the young woman travelled from the fancy California district where she lived to Tucson by Southwest Airlines.

She was used to big buzzing airports like LAX and received her first cultural shock when she touched down in Tucson. The airport was about the size of a shoe box compared to Los Angeles.

The scale of the airport put her in a bad mood "Oh, mercy me, and this is supposed to be the second biggest city in the state, even," she muttered under her breath while leaving the gate.

The airport was not busy at all and she walked briskly toward the luggage belts. The walls were decorated with Southwestern paintings and Native American patterns, but Cheryl had no eye for them. While she stood next to the luggage carousel, she frantically punched her brand-new iPhone and almost missed her red suitcase passing by. She waited for her second case. Just because she had to fulfill a term of studies in "No Man's Land" didn't mean she'd have to look like a country bumpkin hillbilly.

Cheryl always paid attention to her looks, clothes, and makeup. So far, she had not found her Prince Charming but kept her eye out for him. Like most women, she had a taste for fashion and the newest products from the promising cosmetics industry, and appreciated both regularly and well. Dang sure required she keep quite a well-calculated budget each month. The California student didn't expect to meet Mister Perfect in a rustic Western town but had packed wisely nevertheless. Why change old habits?

She was older than most of her fellow students. After a

few years working as an advisor in the unsatisfying world of sales and marketing, she couldn't imagine doing that same job for the rest of her life. She decided on a career in tourism management. That way Cheryl would be able to see unexplored areas of the United States or even different countries. It was high time for a new path in her life. She was in her mid-thirties but didn't look it at all.

An older man in denims and a well-used cowboy hat walked toward her. "Excuse me, are you Cheryl Roberts?"

Cheryl turned, annoyed at first. Who addressed her so bluntly? But then she recalled an email in which the courthouse management had promised to send someone to pick her up. So, she showed her best smile and shook the man's hand.

"That's me! And you are . . .?"

"Bert McEntire, but call me Bert, please. We don't stand much on formalities in Tombstone."

"I bet you don't," Cheryl mumbled as she swung her travel bag around, almost hitting Bert's thigh.

Her luggage was quite a handful but Bert was surprisingly trim and managed without difficulty. They left the arrival terminal, and he walked straight to the opposite parking lot. Cheryl was nearly blinded by the blazing afternoon sun. Bert threw the luggage into his white pickup and started the engine, which came alive with the rumbling sound of an angry cougar. After paying the parking fee at the booth, he drove past the airport motels and onto the interstate.

Cheryl hoped for a decent hotel room in Tombstone, but all she could imagine was a dusty miner's cabin with an outhouse. *God bless*, she thought, already missing her comfortable apartment in Los Angeles. However, what she didn't miss at all was the crazy traffic of the city—six lanes that generally led nowhere, thanks to the daily traffic jams. It was pleasantly calm on the highway leading out of Tucson's suburbs. Compared to Los Angeles, the road toward Cochise County seemed deserted.

Who knows, we might even encounter an old stage coach. She rolled her eyes.

From what Cheryl knew, thanks to Google Maps, the ride would take about an hour. The farther they drove toward Tombstone, the more the scenery changed. It varied from bone-dry desert full of scrubs and thorns to a chain of hills visible at the horizon. Soon they entered the town of Benson, where Bert stopped at a Safeway store. He laughed at Cheryl's puzzled look.

"I thought you might like to buy some groceries. You know, healthy food like cereals, soy milk, salads. Not much of a choice in Tombstone when it comes to grocery shopping, I have to admit. Well, at least we have a Dollar Store now, and, of course, our Circle K gas, station which isn't a real grocery store."

He winked at her, and it was obvious that he was making fun of the California lifestyle of healthy food choices. Bert locked the car, left her luggage on the back seat, and fetched a cart for her. She smiled at his gentlemanly manners.

Oh well, at least there's hope that I might come across some nice-acting people in the next few months. Maybe it won't only be rugged cowboys.

The Benson Safeway was surely not Trader Joe's or Whole Foods, and she already feared for her diet and figure, but at least she was able to buy the necessary stuff. It was actually quite thoughtful of the man to give her the chance to shop for food on the way. But after a few minutes before of the shelves filled with cereals, she turned to Bert and stopped dead in her tracks.

"Wait a minute, how am I going to keep all this in one motel room?" she asked, pointing at her cart which was filling up fast.

He smiled. "Actually, since you'll be staying for a few months, the Parks management organized a small house for you. Cute place. It's an original Victorian from 1881. It belonged to one of the colorful madams from Tombstone's rowdy past."

She must have turned as pale as the eggshell wall in the store, because he quickly assured her that the amenities in the house were, of course, brought up to today's standards. However, Cheryl was not convinced at all and prepared herself for the worst. Hopefully, she wouldn't have to use an outhouse and water pump to shower or wash clothes.

While they drove to their final destination, Bert looked at her. "So, what do you know about Tombstone?"

Cheryl shrugged her shoulders. "Literally nothing," she admitted. "Wait, that's not true. I know that you had some famous gunfight in the 1880s, and Wyatt Earp was staying there and a man called Doc something . . ."

Bert laughed. "Doc Holliday you mean. Yep, that pretty much sums up what most tourists know about Tombstone as well. Well, you'll know much more about the place by the time you leave. I guarantee you that. There's something about Tombstone that sucks you into its history. And believe me, there's so much more history there than that one famous gunfight. It's hard to explain. You have to experience it. One thing is sure, it is a special town and selects the people to whom she shows her true face and history. It seems rather like a village but is far more than just a collection of old buildings."

Cheryl stared at his profile. He spoke about the place as if it were a living person. *Oh Jesus, I'll probably end up with a bunch of cowboy-hat-wearing weirdos around me on a daily basis.* She wasn't really looking forward to the next few months. But what could she do? She needed the internship for her certificate or would fail the entire course.

When they got closer to Tombstone's town limits, Cheryl saw a rugged canyon to the left and asked Bert what the area was called.

"That's Cochise's Stronghold. It's part of the Dragoon Mountains and used to be the hiding spot of the famous Geronimo and Cochise and their renegade band of Chiricahua Apaches. You'd be surprised at the interesting historical places you can find all around Tombstone."

Cheryl had her doubts about that, as she wasn't into frontier history, but didn't want to offend Bert. After all, he'd been very nice to her.

The road they drove on had a few ditches, and numerous hills hid the town until travelers drew quite near. Merely five miles before the city limits, she finally saw Tombstone sitting atop one of the hills. To Cheryl's surprise, there was a checkpoint staged by the local Border Patrol on the left side of the road, and Bert slowed down.

"Wow, are they protecting the town?"

Bert shook his head. "We have many illegal immigrants crossing the border between here and Old Mexico. The Border Patrol fellows try to catch as many as possible and take them back across the border once they've registered the illegals' fingerprints. It's a sad sight and surely doesn't help our tourism at all. The bad part is, many smuggle drugs, and that has quite a tragic impact on society around this area. Some of the drug dealers are quite dangerous, too."

The pretty student studied the guys in uniforms and their threatening-looking dogs waiting patiently in the backs of the patrol cars.

Welcome to the Wild West, she told herself. She stared at the guns and handcuffs attached to the officers' belts.

But the sight was not unknown to her. In California, they had their own share of undocumented migrants and the problems associated with that topic. They drove past the checkpoint and Bert waved at the officers who obviously knew him.

On top of the last hill, the first buildings of their destination welcomed them. To the right they passed two hotels and an RV park, and to the left she saw a sign that read "Boot Hill."

"So you built your cemetery right at the entrance of town? What a welcome for visitors."

Bert looked over at her. "The cemetery is actually a real tourist attraction, as that's where some of the most impressive characters of Tombstone's past are buried."

"Well, as far as I know, neither the Earp brothers nor the notorious Doc Holliday are laid to rest there."

Bert remained silent for a moment. "True, they're not, but their victims surely are. As a matter of fact, Tombstone has two cemeteries."

"You're kidding me. Such a small town has two burial grounds? That seems as if people mainly came here to die in the old days!" It had slipped out of Cheryl's mouth before she realized how rude it may sound. Bert didn't answer right away and she was afraid he was offended.

But then he looked at her and said, "Many died here in the old days and a lot still do. The cause is a similar one. Those days, chances were high to run into a lead bullet, and these days, folks often end up with cancer due to the numerous lead water pipes still being used." With a stern expression, he added "And some folks never leave."

Cheryl found that an utterly strange thing to say, and, goose bumps appeared on her arms. She had no clue what he meant and wasn't about to ask either, for fear of appearing ruder.

They drove around the corner to the Courthouse Museum. It was a lovely Victorian-style brick building, one of the tallest in town. Cheryl loved the white stucco window frames right from the start. Surprisingly, Bert didn't stop at the building but drove a bit farther down the road, stopping in front of a small, cozy-looking Victorian house. It had a nice garden, and a white picket fence lined the perimeter. The center of the front door displayed colorful stained glass with a hummingbird design, and there was a simple rocking chair on the front porch. An archway covered by a lush rose bush in full bloom framed the entrance to the garden. The house was within walking distance to the courthouse, and the road was quiet, not crowded with cars or people. Cheryl loved her temporary domicile the moment she saw it and was anxious to go inside. It almost looked like a doll house, well restored.

As she helped Bert carry some of her luggage onto the porch, the sudden explosion of gunfire made her jump. But he only laughed.

"Don't worry! That was a reenactor in one of the gun shows scaring some tourists. Shooting blanks—no real bullets used, at least most of the time," he added with a boyish grin.

Cheryl nodded. She remembered a Tombstone story in the news about a shooting accident during a celebration of some sort about three years ago. She didn't know if she should be relieved or even more concerned about her stay in this town. It looked like she had arrived right in the middle of some modern version of the "Gun Smoke" television series.

Bert opened the house, handed over the keys and carried her groceries and luggage into the living room and kitchen. Finally, he shook her hand.

"We'll see you tomorrow morning at the museum, then. Come to the front entrance at 9:00 am. Enjoy your first night in Tombstone and get some rest. You must be tired from travelling. Here's my card in case you need anything. Feel free to contact me any time."

"Thank you so much for your kindness, Bert. I'll see you tomorrow." He waved, jumped into his pickup truck, and drove off.

CHAPTER 3

***

CHERYL WALKED THROUGH WHAT WOULD BE HER TEMPORARY HOME FOR THE next few months to come. It was small, alright, but it was definitely much better than having a tiny one-room hotel accommodation. At least she had enough space to put away all her clothes and prepare herself a meal. There was a small living room, a tiny kitchen, and a cozy bedroom. The bathroom was small but very cute, with an old-fashioned, claw-footed bathtub, which also offered the possibility of taking a shower behind a lace-covered shower curtain.

The interior of the house was decorated with antique furniture. A lot of pictures on the walls showed scenes from the once-so-glorious past of Tombstone. For an instant Cheryl wondered what it had been like in those days. Although she was very much into modern architecture, she somehow liked the charming place right from the minute she set a foot in it. Strangely, the furniture seemed almost familiar to her, and she loved the creaking hardwood floor. She could really dig this place for the next few months. Whether she could get used to the Western town itself was a completely different story. Her doubts about that remained. But since the accommodation felt comfortable, she began to open up to the fact that she could spend the next four-to-five months here. The eager student was actually looking forward to her first day at work now.

Cheryl put away her groceries in the kitchen and started the coffee machine right away. What would she do without coffee? Her friends in California always made fun of her, calling her a coffee junkie. Most likely they were right about that.

She hauled the heavy luggage into the small bedroom and started unpacking her clothes.

Meanwhile, the delicious aroma of the brewing coffee wafted through the entire house like an exquisite perfume. It was quite a challenge for her to stow all her belongings without creating a picture of absolute chaos in the bedroom.

Once she was done, the place almost looked like a real home. She poured herself a big mug of coffee and sat in the rocking chair outside on the porch, savoring the taste of the hot beverage. It was time to unwind from the tough day.

So, this was Tombstone. She glanced up and down the street. It was a quiet town. No cars drove along this side street at the moment, and the gun shows were done for the day. The temperature cooled down and she watched the magnificent colors of the sun set. The sudden chill Cheryl felt surprised her despite the previous heat of the day.

But then she remembered Tombstone's high elevation and went inside, grabbed a shawl to wrap around her shoulders, and refilled her cup. The pretty woman returned to the porch and enjoyed the evening. Sudden movement caught her eye and almost caused her to spill the coffee. She couldn't believe it.

A deer stood only a few feet away, watching her. "Hello, John Deer," she called out and laughed at her own joke.

Cheryl yawned and decided to call it a day. Exploring the town would have to wait until later this week. She was tired from travelling and went inside for a shower. After all, a new job waited for her the next day even if it was only a temporary one.

Before she crawled under the bed covers, Cheryl turned off the air conditioning. It was a simple unit but it worked well and kept the small house cool during the day. She didn't need the AC in the evening as the temperature dropped almost as much as it did back home in L.A. No doubt it the air was dry here too.

The house had stone walls, and the way they functioned to keep the place cool in the climate was simply amazing. One thing was sure, the air here was much cleaner compared to the polluted layer over L.A.

Cheryl snuggled deeper into the cozy blanket that lay across the old-fashioned iron bed and looked around the room. Its appearance resembled the perfect image of a Victorian era magazine. Strung crystals dangled from the shade of the lamp on the nightstand, causing hundreds of shiny little stars to reflect onto the old-fashioned floral wallpaper. The place was absolutely lovely. You could almost call it romantic. And with that thought, Cheryl turned off the light and drifted into a deep slumber.

***

Late at night, a lonely coyote screeched on one of the hills, calling for his mate. It was far past midnight. The main museum room of the Bird Cage Theatre lay in darkness. Only the emergency exit lights produced a weak green gleam around the stairs leading through the different sections of the theater. The old piano stood silent in front of the big stage with its old dusty, faded curtain. The building was cool inside, thanks to the adobe walls.

To protect the countless artifacts of Tombstone's glorious past, it was strictly prohibited to smoke in the building. Everything inside the different rooms was dry as bones in the desert except for the bottles of old beverages that stood on the shelf of the antique bar near the entrance of the famous establishment. The darkness inside made it impossible for anyone to peer through the windows late at night, hence nobody witnessed the thick cigar smoke swirling toward the ceiling.

Thanks to the dimness, not a single person could see the beverages in the bottles kept for decoration gently swaying from side to side as if a drink had just been poured. The Bird Cage was alive.

CHAPTER 4

***

THE NEXT MORNING CHERYL WOKE EARLY AND STRETCHED, LINGERING UNDER the warm covers a few more moments. She had had some weird dreams about long calico dresses and old saloon music, but nevertheless, felt relaxed. It was time for coffee and some oatmeal, and off she would be to her first day at the Courthouse Museum.

Cheryl dressed in her favorite denims and a fancy blouse, brushed her hair, and added light daytime make-up which emphasized her dark green eyes. Then she walked over to the museum, arriving ten minutes early just as Bert McEntire turned the corner.

"Howdy, Miss Roberts." He greeted her in a friendly manner and tipped his cowboy hat.

"Call me Cheryl, if you don't mind."

"Okay, Cheryl, then. Hey, I hope you slept well? Here comes my wife Dorothea."

"Yes, I did. I love that little house. It's so cute, and all the antiques add to its charm in a special way."

A woman in her late fifties walked toward them and started to talk with quite a raspy voice. "I'm glad you enjoy the interior of the place. Actually, some of the furniture belonged to my great-grandmother who ran one of the houses of ill repute here in town. She was French. By the way, I'm Dorothea McEntire. Pleasure to meet you, Cheryl!"

Cheryl liked Bert's wife immediately. Her face was weathered from working in the sun, her handshake was firm, and her smile warm and welcoming.

"Let me show you around, and then I'll explain what your job for today will be until you know the museum a bit better." So the student from California dutifully followed Dorothea McEntire.

"You can leave your bag in the room behind our cashier booth. Nobody has access there but us. I'll give you a quick tour through the museum. Of course, you can have a closer look at the objects in the late afternoon. I suggest you stay with me in the booth today so you can handle the admission fee the visitors have to pay. Not much to learn for that. Pretty easy to operate our credit card terminal. But first, a quick round through our lovely courthouse."

Dorothea smiled and winked at Cheryl who followed, smiling back at her. The first chamber to the right showed smaller artifacts. According to the signs, some of them had even belonged to the famous Wyatt Earp, like his pocket watch and a personal straight razor. She would have to check them out later. Dorothea and her trainee walked from room to room. The museum had many items displayed from Tombstone's colorful past. There were a lot of mining tools and equipment, horse buggies, weapons, even an original courtroom arranged with all its antique furniture and bookshelves. The younger woman wondered what kind of trials had been held here in the old days.

Household items, ranching equipment, a safe—you name it and it was there, displayed nicely in different showcases or on pedestals. The courthouse was more or less like a color picture book of Tombstone's heyday. To her surprise, Cheryl was looking forward to exploring all of the artifacts during the next few weeks. She had never been into Wild West history but somehow this small museum drew her to learn more about it. After all, she had to write a huge essay about her training experience here. It would be ideal to find a specific topic to write about. She was astonished she felt interested in the history now, merely twenty-four hours after arrival in a town she hadn't even wanted to be in to begin with.

But Cheryl had decided to make the best out of the situation and to learn as much as possible for her studies. After all, she was the ambitious type of student.

Dorothea explained the cashier equipment and which fees to charge for the different visitors. She was a humble and patient teacher and it didn't take long for Cheryl to manage the cash register alone while Dorothea handled a group of visitors, guiding them through the place.

Around lunch time, Bert came by with a basket of fresh sandwiches, cold bottles of Mountain Dew soda, and Dorothea had the coffee maker running. To her surprise, they shared their lunch with Cheryl.

One thing is sure, they are really nice people and not so selfish like the city people tend to be, Cheryl mused while chewing on a delicious turkey sandwich. What surprised her even more was the rich taste of the coffee Bert offered.

He laughed. "It's Arbuckle coffee, my dear, real cowboy coffee with a long history."

Cheryl nodded. "I dang sure could get used to this brew."

The three laughed. After half an hour they went back to work, and the afternoon went by quickly. The place wasn't busy on this weekday and Dorothea encouraged

Cheryl to take a stroll alone through the entire museum in the late afternoon.

Cheryl walked from room to room and admired the old furniture and items in the showcases. She was astonished at how many chemicals had been used for silver processing in the old days, and how much medical equipment was displayed. It was originally used by a doctor named Goodfellow. Cheryl laughed at the name. But it seemed that he had been a doctor with very advanced knowledge considering the medical standards those days. He even did surgeries right here in this small town.

She thought about how it must have been to undergo a gunshot wound surgery without today's medical procedures. The thought left her shivering.

Exploring more rooms led her upstairs to the second floor where she stood awestruck next to the beautifully crafted wooden stairway. The stairs were worn and scratched but still beautiful, and the banisters felt so smooth under her touch. After strolling through every upstairs chamber, Cheryl couldn't help but admire how amazingly the museum was equipped. Obviously, people had put in a lot of passion and love for the town's history.

The sun was already setting when Cheryl Roberts walked toward the side entrance close to the courtroom that led into the backyard of the museum. To her surprise, she saw ropes dangling from gallows. Cheryl shuddered in spite of the last rays of warm sun.

So even hangings took place here? Maybe it's just a decoration. I'll ask Bert about it.

As she turned to find Bert standing right behind her, she jumped. He slowly nodded and answered her unspoken question right away.

"Yes, Cheryl, seven men were hanged in this courtyard

over the years. Tombstone was the county seat of Cochise for quite a few years; therefore, trials and executions were held right here. Saved folks the long ride to Tucson. Sometimes, you might still witness a man dangling on one of those ropes."

Cheryl thought the man was pulling her leg but she saw he was dead serious. *No pun intended.* She didn't dare laugh.

Walking back into the museum, she noticed the sunset behind the courthouse was a beautiful sight but didn't look back over her shoulder.

In the evening Cheryl walked along famous Allen Street, the center of Tombstone's tourist attractions. She decided to celebrate her arrival in the "Wild West" with a juicy steak at the Longhorn Restaurant which Bert had highly recommended.

It was interesting to walk along the boardwalk and glance into the tourist shop windows. The two major saloons weren't busy, but it was still early. *People probably don't go out much on a Thursday evening.*

Her dinner at the Longhorn was delicious. Cheryl read the friendly, older server's name tag: "Donna." It was as though the two had known each other for years. In Los Angeles, Cheryl was well used to the anonymous treatment but in this Western restaurant, she enjoyed the humble friendliness.

The sizzling steak, baked potato, and homemade coleslaw were mouthwatering. Cheryl was so full she told the waitress that Donna would have to roll her down the street. She paid and walked back to her little Victorian accommodation enjoying the cool evening air after the very filling dinner.

As Cheryl arrived at her temporary home she decided to

hang out on the porch for a little while. She watched two deer trotting along the road toward the RV Park, probably on the hunt for food. Looking to the sky, Cheryl realized she had never seen so many stars in the night like here in Tombstone. The Milky Way showed perfectly in all its beauty. One hardly ever saw stars in L.A. due to the hundred thousand streetlights.

Also, the quiet was a new experience for her. Cheryl would have never believed it if someone had told her so before, but she enjoyed the silence and the darkness enveloping her.

She studied the night sky and was suddenly surprised to hear a soft whisper. "Mae!" Cheryl looked around, but no one could be seen.

Maybe sounds from down the street playing tricks on my mind. Relaxing again, she moved the rocking chair back and forth to a rhythmic, but creaky sound. The voice sounded again. "Mae, come to me, my love!"

Cheryl earnestly searched the darkness. Still, no one was visible in front of the house. She shook her head and went inside. *My ears must be playing tricks on me. This city girl is just not used to the desert. Or maybe it was that big dinner lulling me into dreamland.*

CHAPTER 5

* * *

DELICATE RAYS OF SILVER MOONLIGHT BATHED THE SLEEPING TOWN. AT HALF past two in the morning, the theater sat on the end of the street, waiting for its guests as it always had since it first opened in the winter of 1881.

A soft whisper murmured from a booth above the stage. "She's back just as she promised so many decades ago. Mae has returned. I won't let her go this time. She belongs to me. She belongs to Tombstone."

The deep, pleasant voice faded into the darkness, with the aroma of cherry cigars. He was not in a hurry for her to return and had waited over one hundred thirty years within the old walls. To him, it only felt like days. Waiting a bit longer wouldn't matter. After all, he had eternity on his side. She would find her way to him—he was certain of that.

Cheryl slept but frightening dreams of gallows with ropes swaying in a gentle breeze haunted her. The next morning, she yawned and felt tired despite her eight hours of sleep. With a second cup of strong coffee, she tried her best to hide how dragged out she felt upon arriving at the museum. Cheryl didn't want to appear moody with her new bosses or the tourist visitors.

The following days went by so fast. The Courthouse Museum was busier on the weekends, and Cheryl's evenings were occupied with taking notes for the essay and studying her tourism management books. There was a lot of noise coming from the saloons on Friday and Saturday nights, and Cheryl avoided them since they were mostly packed with drunken men. Some women too—the ones who wanted to show off or act tough.

She wasn't into drinking and knew how alcohol can change people's behavior, most times not for the better.

On Monday, Dorothea invited Cheryl to accompany her to buy some groceries in the city of Sierra Vista about 20 miles from Tombstone, and Cheryl gladly accepted. It was nice to get out of town for a little while, and stocking up on groceries was a good idea since she couldn't afford eating at restaurants every day. It would shrink her budget much too quickly. Dorothea showed her everything available in Sierra Vista, even a hairdresser, which would come in handy. The student enjoyed the woman's company a great deal. The older lady seemed to be more sophisticated than Cheryl had first expected.

"Have you always lived in Tombstone, Dorothea?" Cheryl hoped she wasn't being too nosy, but wondered how one could live a whole lifetime in a small town. Dorothea shook her head.

"You may not believe it, but we used to live right in the center of San Diego."

The girl from California was a bit shocked, and her eyebrows raised. "What in the world made you move to a small settlement like Tombstone?"

"Well, the first time we set foot in town was during a vacation trip with our RV over twenty years ago. We had toured pretty much all of Arizona and Utah. The Grand Canyon, Bryce Canyon, Arches National Park—we've seen it all. On the way back to San Diego we decided to take the southern route and stopped here. We got hooked right from the first minute we arrived. The history is fascinating. It's difficult to explain but there is something about Tombstone that doesn't let go of you. It's like stepping back in time. We returned often after that first stay, and when Bert retired from his engineering job we finally decided to move here.

"Good part is, it's much cheaper to live here than in San Diego. Then, two years after we moved here, the position as director of the museum became available and we decided to go for it. But once a year we still take a vacation with our RV.

"I have to admit that California has become way too hectic and crowded for us. We'll never be tempted to return there to live. We'd rather go to Utah or New Mexico, even Colorado. No, my dear, I don't miss California at all."

I could never imagine living in a town the size of a small village. I need the California culture, sports facilities, day spas, shopping centers, Hollywood, and all the fancy restaurants. I'd probably die of boredom if I had to live in a place like Tombstone for good. Not to mention all the gossip that follows people's every move when living in such a tiny community. I love the lifestyle of a big city.

Maybe the crime is bad, and the traffic, and the pollution is disgusting. And Dorothea was right about the exorbitant cost of living there. But you can't have all the amenities without the negative stuff. There's always good with the bad.

The two women enjoyed a salad together, some iced tea, and went shopping for groceries after lunch. Cheryl was surprised at the many choices of European food in the store and Dorothea explained that the variety was available thanks to the Fort Huachuca military base. Apparently, the army guys brought their taste for different specialties from all over the world. And sometimes they brought a wife from overseas. No wonder one could find Polish sausages, German dark bread, or even smoked Black Forest ham in the local grocery stores.

On the way back they chatted about the house where Cheryl was staying.

"I really love it. It's super cute, and although small, it's really cozy."

Dorothea nodded. "It was the living quarters of a real madam of Tombstone's red-light district. She was one of my ancestors." Cheryl blushed but Dorothea laughed.

"There's nothing to feel ashamed about. Those days, women didn't have much of a choice to earn their own money. There was a big demand for ladies of the line in Tombstone, actually across the whole frontier. Females were highly outnumbered. Therefore, the miners and gamblers, gunfighters, and cowboys, would pay any price for a lady's affection, even if she was no lady at all. To a certain extent, you might say that men knew the value of a woman better in those days than they do now. No wonder many women went for that source of steady income. Some had a choice, but most had none."

Cheryl had never thought of it from this point of view and she had to agree with Dorothea.

"In case you're worried, I can reassure you that Crazy Anne never performed her trade in the house where you are staying. Rather, she managed one of the brothels in town. Well-known as a 'calico queen,' she mainly performed at the Bird Cage Theatre up on Allen Street."

"Performed?"

Dorothea smiled.

"Yes, she ran a group of can-can dancers and they did quite daring choreographies in very revealing costumes, if you want to believe the history books."

Cheryl was amazed at the woman's extensive knowledge about the town's past and its red-light district.

"You know, Girl, sometimes this town doesn't offer you much of a choice. It confronts you with its colorful history sooner or later when you least expect it. Tombstone has a way of communicating with some people in quite outstanding, sometimes tragic ways."

Cheryl had no clue what she meant and waited for further explanation but it didn't come. Dorothea dropped the subject as fast as it had come up.

The rest of the day went by quickly and, for her taste, too soon Cheryl found herself standing in front of her guest house again when Dorothea dropped her off. Groceries in hand, she waved goodnight to her new friend.

It had been a nice day. She stacked away the food she had bought and was looking forward to the increased variety for dinner in her fridge. She brewed a cup of her beloved coffee and sat outside on her rocking chair which was fast becoming her favorite spot of the house.

The sun set in gorgeous crimson and orange colors, and a lonely coyote yipped from between the hills far behind the garden. Cheryl felt content, although she remembered grumbling in the beginning about being assigned to Tombstone. Now she loved this homely little place where she lived for the time being. Yes, it somehow strangely felt like home.

CHAPTER 6

***

LISA LEFT THE SALOON LATER THAN USUAL, AND DESPITE HER NORMAL ROUTINE to avoid the direct route from Big Nose Kate's to her parking space at the bottom of the hill behind the Bird Cage Theatre, she walked right by the dark building this time.

"Screw this dang old brothel," she mumbled under her breath. She wanted to get home.

Dead tired, her feet were throbbing. She worked a double shift because one of the bartenders had called in sick with the flu barely an hour before his shift started, so Lisa had to stay behind another five endless hours. She was angry with her boss for demanding that from her, but needed the job and did not dare refuse taking on the extra time. At least Lisa made a good number of tips today. Her fiancé was most likely upset with her now since she had to call off their date for a movie over in Sierra Vista.

Passing the main entrance of the dark building at a brisk stride, she heard a moaning sound. *Must be the old adobe structure groaning because of the late-night temperature drop*, she thought.

That happened quite often in the old structures along

the main tourist street. It didn't worry her much. Around the corner toward the back side of the museum, it was too dark to make out her car. *That darn city council needs to come up with the additional streetlights they promised, all the way to the parking area so I could find my car.*

"Dang, if it was mainly for the tourists, the silly lights would shine all over the place like a freaking Christmas tree," she cursed and was fed up with searching her way with the dim light of her cell phone.

"A silver dollar should be enough for you, little bird!"

Lisa spun around, nearly losing her balance on those stupid stilettos while she tried to figure out where the voice had come from. She wasn't in the mood for a bad joke pulled by some drunken coward hiding behind a corner. She glanced back at Allen Street but no one was there. So she shook her head and was just about to continue her walk toward the car when she heard the voice again.

"Come on over. I said, I'll pay you well!"

Lisa looked over her shoulder again, worried now. Cold sweat covered her forehead.

"Who are you? I've got mace and I'm calling 911."

No answer. The waitress turned around, ready to run. As she passed the rear wall of the former brothel, an old wooden door opened. In all the years Lisa had been working at Big Nose Kate's, she had never realized there was another door into the historical building. But before she could consider it, she was yanked back brutally by a steely grip at her neck, and pulled into the building. She tried to fight the dark shadow of a man she had never seen before, frantically trying to get away. But she didn't have a chance. The door closed behind her with a shrieking noise. Her screams in the depths of the museum's basement remained unheard above in the streets of Tombstone. Nobody saw what happened. No soul came to help her.

The next morning tourists and locals drove down the hill behind the town's center and parked next to Lisa's little red car. The day promised to be a bustling one.

As people walked by the building known as a historic brothel and saloon, they didn't pay any attention to the rear wall. It was only an adobe wall, old with its fading color chipping off. Nothing to see there except for some bushy grass. The main entrance to the Bird Cage faced Allen Street, and the backside of it offered neither an entrance nor an exit for its visitors.

The owner of Big Nose Kate's saloon was angry with his employees.

"At least John, the bartender, had the guts to call in sick. Lisa is probably so mad at me for having to work his shift after her own that she doesn't even call to let me know where the heck she is. Simply doesn't show up for work. Can you believe that? Man, I tell you, it gets harder and harder to find decent employees."

His friend at the bar sipped his fresh coffee and nodded in agreement. He ran the shop opposite the saloon and had seen his share of unreliable employees over the years. He gulped the rest of his beverage, and they both wished each other a successful morning. While the saloon owner watched him walk across the street to open his souvenir shop, he still cussed and grumbled about Lisa not showing up for work.

No one heard anything from her over the next 48 hours while her little red car sat lonely and shimmering in the day's heat on the parking lot.

And nobody caught the shiny reflection of her car keys in the stubby, dry grass at the wall of the backside of the old structure.

CHAPTER 7

***

CHERYL HAD BEEN IN TOWN FOR MORE THAN THREE WEEKS. SHE HAD LEARNED about the famous gunfight at the O.K. Corral between the Earp brothers, Doc Holliday, and a gang of cowboys. By now she also knew some facts about the notorious Doc Holliday and somehow couldn't help but wonder what the men involved in that deadly conflict so many years ago would say if they knew how their killing reputation was still being celebrated nowadays. A lot of people even saw them as national heroes.

In Cheryl's eyes it was not a heroic story, but rather the gunfight was merely the logical consequence of a long-term, smoldering conflict back in a time when men wore weapons and used them to end an argument.

She shook her head in disbelief when she saw modern men, reenactors they were called, dressed up as Wyatt Earp, Doc Holliday, or Curly Bill. They seemed to live their role rather than just dressing up like those gunfighters from the days long gone.

Cheryl had visited the saloons and liked their atmosphere but avoided them during the weekends. Too many drunks tried to get "funny" with her—obnoxious, really. She was seen as the new kid in town and quite a few tried to hit on her. But none of the men held any interest for Cheryl. She preferred the educated ones and, if possible, good looking or at least well dressed. And there was something else. Cheryl had a taste for long, wavy hair. She didn't know where that preference came from but she had always had it.

Nowadays, it seemed that most men sported a military like haircut, or even shaved heads, very much to Cheryl's distaste. She could daydream for hours about the long hair of a secret lover caressing her naked skin.

She quickly shook off the romantic thoughts. It was time to close the museum for the day. Cheryl had decided to take an evening stroll around the area that had once been known as the red-light district in the old days.

She had done a fair amount of reading lately and, for some reason, was fascinated by the past about the shady ladies in this town. Students in her program had to write a long essay to graduate so she decided to write about the topic of the fallen angels of Tombstone. Dorothea had generously lent her a whole stack of books about the soiled doves which could be well used for her studies.

Cheryl had become close friends with the McEntire couple. Despite the age difference, she liked both of them very much for their wit, humor, and high level of education. Sometimes they met for a relaxed evening of barbecuing together.

Well, maybe being assigned to the Tombstone out-post isn't that bad after all. On her porch she enjoyed a sandwich made with fresh-sliced turkey and a glass of homemade lemonade.

She put her plate and glass in the sink, took her cozy wool shawl, and left the house. She knew once the sun sets at this higher elevation it gets chilly pretty fast.

It was different to walk the streets of Tombstone at twilight. She strolled much slower and at a more leisurely pace than her normal sporty stride. As she passed Sixth Street where the red-light district's center used to be in the old days, the sudden aroma of cherry cigars filled the air. Cheryl looked over her shoulder but nobody was there.

Must have been from a person walking along this street before me. Cheryl inhaled deeply and immediately liked the cherry flavored tobacco, although she had never smoked her entire life. It was a pleasant aroma and seemed somewhat familiar. As she continued to walk, the cigar smell followed her.

Probably my nose starting to play funny games because of all the mesquite bushes around here.

She walked by a building on the left and decided to cut over to Allen Street, as the small road ahead of her seemed to be leading right into the dusty hills outside of Tombstone's town limits. Cheryl turned left and walked by an adobe building she did not know.

A sudden pain made her groan. It was like the stab of a knife at her temples and when she closed her eyes green sparks appeared behind her closed eyelids. She started to feel dizzy and had to touch the wall next to her to steady herself. A weird tingle spread from her fingertips, and the hand touching the wall went numb. The smell of cherry cigars was almost overwhelming. It felt like she was going to faint.

"Mae, my sunshine! Mae!"

She recognized the voice from the other night on her porch. The numbness in her hand spread further up her arm.

"Miss, are you okay? Can I help you?"

The young biker looked at the pale woman leaning

against the wall. At first, he had been annoyed, thinking she was nothing but a drunk, but then he saw perspiration covering her face and that she was pale as a ghost despite her summer tan. Something was wrong with her, so he decided to help. He touched her arm gently, just in time to catch her as she fainted.

"Probably dehydrated," he mumbled while he carried her toward a bench on the opposite side of the main boardwalk. He removed a water bottle from his backpack and poured some cool water into his palm to refresh her sweaty face.

She woke feeling confused. "Where am I?"

"You fainted. I'd better bring you to your hotel or wherever you're staying. Do you need a doctor?"

She shook her head. "No, thank you. I'm feeling better already."

"Okay. I'll walk you back to your place to make sure you don't fall or faint again." Cheryl nodded and thanked the young man.

Behind the wall of the adobe building, an angry scream erupted into the darkness of the building. "She's mine. I will bring her back!"

A dark shape of a pale woman held out a silver dollar coin toward the direction of the angry voice. Her blood red lipstick emphasized the grotesque mask her face had turned into. The inhabitants of the building had given her a new name. She was "Silver Dollar Elisabeth" now.

But Cheryl was unaware of all this as she thanked the young man who walked her home. She offered him some lemonade but he refused.

"Time to hit the road with the bike, getting dark pretty fast. See you around town sometime. I work at the Four Deuces Saloon down the road. My name is Morgan."

"Thank you, Morgan. I really appreciate your help. I

don't know what came over me. See you around town."

She waved goodbye as he walked down the road toward the saloon where she assumed he most likely had parked his motorcycle.

He looks sad, head hanging down. Nice fellow. Attractive, too. Poor guy, must be depressed about something.

Cheryl had no clue what had happened during her walk uptown. The sudden migraine was gone and the numbness in her arm, too. How weird. She sat on her rocking chair sipping her second glass of lemonade, trying to rest. She felt a bit weak, tired, and decided to call it an early night and get some rest.

As she turned toward the front door, the faint smell of cherry cigars caressed her nostrils again. *I must be imagining things. Just exhausted, I guess.* She went inside and headed for bed.

Curls of cigar smoke rose into the cool night air as a dark shadow leaned against the pole on Cheryl's front porch. The woman slept soundly and dreamlessly in her beautiful Victorian iron framed bed on the other side of the wall.

CHAPTER 8

***

THE NEXT MORNING A POLICE SEARCH WAS THE TALK OF THE TOWN WHEN CHERYL arrived at the museum. She felt refreshed from a good night's rest and decided to buy some migraine medication at the Dollar Store later, in case yesterday's headache should return. When Cheryl saw the sheriff and two Arizona rangers talking with the McEntires, she walked toward them, wondering what the fuss was all about.

The sheriff tipped his hat.

"Good morning, ma'am. May we ask you some questions?"

Cheryl looked puzzled and shrugged her shoulders.

"Sure, go ahead."

One of the rangers unfolded a print of a woman in her early thirties with blond hair and heavy makeup. "Have you seen this lady in the past few days?" the sheriff asked.

Cheryl thought the face looked familiar. After a minute she knew where she had seen her. "I saw her at Big Nose Kate's Saloon a few days ago. Why?"

One of the rangers gave her a sheriff's office business card. "Her name is Lisa Callaghan. She's missing, but her car is still parked in town. Disappeared three days ago after her evening shift. If you see or hear anything from her, let us know please."

Disappeared? A cold chill caused Cheryl to rub her arms. It was surely not the kind of news one would expect in a small town like Tombstone.

"Maybe she ran off with a handsome guy?"

The sheriff shook his head at that suggestion. "No way. She's Morgan's girlfriend. The guy who bartends at the Four Deuces. He's looked all over Cochise County for her. They were planning to get married in two months. No, Lisa would not run away with some other fellow. She might be grumpy from time to time, but is head over heels for Morgan and, as far as I know, he's madly in love with her, too. We questioned him already. He's devastated and has no clue as to her whereabouts."

Cheryl remembered the sad expression on the young guy's face yesterday. *No wonder he seemed so depressed. So, it was your girlfriend that disappeared. Where in the world would she go?* Cheryl walked into the Courthouse Museum deep in thought.

Lisa remained the main topic in town for a few days. Some assumed she had run away with some other cowboy, maybe chickening out of the wedding. Some thought that Morgan had something to do with her disappearance.

Just as the local authorities were about to give up the search for Lisa, her car keys were found close to her car behind the Bird Cage. Now the talk about the presumed crime scared not only some of the tourists when they heard about it, but many female locals as well. Was it safe to walk the streets of Tombstone at night?

As Cheryl and Dorothea enjoyed their Mexican dinner at Margarita's Restaurant, Dorothea seemed thoughtful and more silent than usual. Cheryl asked if something was wrong, and after a brief hesitation, her new friend spoke, her voice barely a whisper.

"You know, Lisa is not the first woman to have disappeared in this town."

"What do you mean?" Cheryl asked, setting her fork down.

"Well, I did a lot of research on the town's history, partly for the museum and partly out of my own personal interest.

I came across similar stories of women who had disappeared in Tombstone throughout the past few decades. Some were not taken seriously, as some of the women had ... had ... well, let's say, a less-than-spotless reputation. So far, there are three ladies missing, if you want to include Lisa. Four women that vanished into thin air. The police were never able to press charges, as they never found any bodies or evidence of a crime, but, hell, this whole area is full of mining shafts. It would not be a difficult task at all to have a corpse disappear for good without leaving a trace."

Cheryl was shocked. She might've expected such news in L.A. but not here in a small Western community in such a remote location. Dorothea studied the food on her plate for a few moments. When she spoke again, her voice was sad.

"What I found out is that the women started disappearing after the mines closed, along with the boomtown entertainment such as the Bird Cage Brothel and Saloon in 1889. Right after the heyday of the silver boom. First, I thought it might be one man repeatedly kidnapping girls, but there are many years between the incidents, so it can hardly be one guy responsible for all of the crimes. And the sad part is, as long as there's no evidence and no skeletons, the police and the FBI couldn't follow the few facts they had. The cases closed, or at least became 'cold' and have never been solved.

"They found no traces of the women after they vanished, but they all have one thing in common. All of them worked in Tombstone saloons and all disappeared between late evening and twilight of the next morning."

Chills ran up and down Cheryl's spine and she sat stone-faced. *Was it possible? The touristy Western heritage town was the seat of such crime?*

Cheryl decided to do some research to find out more about Tombstone's earlier history after the famous gunfight at the O.K. Corral. She would start at the only place she had not visited yet, the Bird Cage Theatre itself.

Scheduled to be off work the following day, Cheryl decided to pay a visit to the tourist attraction, now a well-known museum and must-see spot, according to most townsfolk. She decided to go right after breakfast, as she wanted to avoid the tourist crowds and have a look undisturbed. All Cheryl knew about the place was that it had been a brothel, a saloon and gambling establishment more than a theater, and not a family entertainment place as it might have been in modern times.

A memory flashed of how she had fainted behind the building only a few days before. This time she was prepared with a bottle of water and candy bar in her purse. *Maybe it was just low blood sugar.*

The lady at the front entrance who ran the day shift gave her a friendly greeting. "Hey, so finally you come to visit our museum. Welcome! I'm Heather." Apparently, the news about Cheryl working at the Courthouse Museum must have travelled fast around town.

"I'm Cheryl. Pleasure to meet you, Heather."

"Well, let me know if you need any information. I

haven't started the cash register yet but I'll give you a free ticket today. After all, you may be able to promote us among the courthouse visitors. You know how it is, one hand washes the other."

"That's very kind of you and yes, I will most likely come back with lots of questions for my studies. And, of course I'll tell people about the famous Bird Cage Theatre."

"Feel free to ask as much as you want, sweetie." Heather handed Cheryl a ticket while pointing the way into the main museum room.

The early visitor remained in the front room for a few minutes and marveled at the beautifully tooled bar made from a dark hardwood and the mirror behind it with the shelves full of antique liquor bottles. A small staircase at the other end of the room led upstairs to a gallery under the wooden ceiling of the theater. She slowly walked toward the well-worn steps, and suddenly shivered as though something, or someone, was holding her back from moving any closer.

"These were the stairs leading up to the so-called cribs. The girls would go up there to entertain quite differently than the girls on the stage, if you know what I mean."

Heather laughed and winked. "Actually, it was cheap money up there, mainly dirty miners and sweaty cowboys looking for some female affection. The ones that were better off had the pleasure of booking the beautiful women in the downstairs brothel," Heather explained.

Cheryl stared at Heather. "You mean there were differ-ent classes of prostitutes?"

Heather nodded. "Oh, yes, dear. The ones who were young, pretty, and smart actually could make a real fortune as soiled doves in Tombstone. But the older ones or the unattractive ones, the Chinese or Mexican prostitutes …

sadly, they were often abused and for very low pay. Most of them either fell sick with diseases or committed suicide by drinking poison. But, as I said, some were almost like movie stars of today and earned big bucks."

Cheryl was fascinated and looked around at all the items in the saloon entry area. She saw some sort of an antique music box and a big oil painting of an exotic dancer with three breasts.

Heather pointed at the picture. "Meet Fatima, Little Egypt. She was indeed a belly dancer who performed here in the old days. If she really had three breasts, I can't say. We never found proof of it. But she was indeed a true, living performer at our establishment. One thing is sure, this town has seen a lot of strange things since its founding."

Cheryl thanked Heather and turned to the door leading to the main museum room. Stepping through the tiny doorway, she noticed how dark and cool it was. When the door closed behind her, she felt as if she was being swallowed into the vacuum of a long-forgotten time. She glanced around but didn't know where to begin.

On the other side of the room she saw a stage framed with an old, dusty curtain, its golden fringes dangling. The burgundy color was faded as it hung sadly from the high ceiling. An old piano stood silently in front of the stage. Toward the ceiling "cribs" faced the stage and the center of the room. The cribs were compact chambers sparsely furnished with a simple bed and a faded blanket. A petroleum lamp once provided a dim light. There was barely enough space to walk around the bed, but the miners must not have cared about that.

The museum had illuminated the cribs with small spotlights and decorated them with wallpaper of different designs. Some of it had started to peel off the walls. Faded velvet curtains hung on either side of the cribs. Water stains from leaks and countless small holes were visible on the wooden ceiling.

My God, those must be bullet holes. Her brain conjured an image of people wildly shooting at each other and toward the ceiling, maybe to let off drunken steam. *That must have been insane! How could they have taken such a risk in a crowded room?*

Shaking her head in disbelief, she looked at what was displayed in the showcases. Beautiful items—from medical instruments to porcelain plates, silver cutlery, weapons, and even an old gambling table. The room was full of different artifacts. Clothes, old music instruments, and guns—all of them whispered of the old days and their heroes and villains.

There was a faro table that had been, according to the printed sign, used by Doc Holliday himself. Cheryl moved steadily toward the piano in the center of the room. Softly pressing on the keys, a faint, mistuned tone sounded. The keys felt strange, and she sensed a tingle as if the piano were caressing her back. Cheryl quickly pulled back her hand, which had grown cold.

At her left was a small stair leading behind the stage. A single booth next to the stairs, the only one at base level, housed a little table, a single wooden chair, a deck of poker cards, and a bottle of whiskey, all seemingly waiting for the next person willing to gamble. Cheryl closed her eyes as the scent of cherry cigar smoke engulfed her.

When she opened her eyes again, she still stood in front of the piano, yet, by God, the place was not the same. It was loud and smoke drifted in thick layers through the room. The whole place was crowded with people, mostly men in frontier-styled clothes. The air bore the stench of sweat, cigar smoke, and gun powder. The piano played a lively polka song and the establishment bustled with the noise of cheerful female laughter and husky male voices. The clinking of glasses from men toasting each other rang in her ears. A singing voice accompanied the piano. Cheryl looked at the entertainer who wore a daring, low-cut, red dress.

She stared at the woman whose hair was pinned up with beautiful ivory combs. Her face had been powdered a ghostly white, her cheeks and lips colored red. The fact that Cheryl was able to see the dusty curtain of the stage shimmering through the lady's body made her skin crawl with fear.

Where did all these people come from all of a sudden? She had entered the room alone, and now it was packed with folks in strange attire. *What in the world is happening? Low blood sugar again?* When she turned her head away from the stage toward the single poker booth she stared right into his face. Long, light brown hair fell over his shoulders, his well-trimmed mustache almost hid the curve of his smiling lips as he looked at her, his steely gray-blue eyes showing an amused twinkle.

"Hello Mae. Finally, you are here again, my love! I have waited so long for you."

Cheryl didn't feel the hardness of the floor in front of the poker booth. She was unconscious before she came struck it.

CHAPTER 9

***

Mae got off the stagecoach. Oh, how she hated to travel these god-forsaken dirt trails on the stage lines.

Not only was this dangerous territory packed with outlaws and renegade Apaches, but one could break every dang bone in one's body because of the stage's constant and wild jolting up and down and back and forth. She felt as though everyplace on her body was bruised by the time she got off the coach. But she had no choice. The carnival group with which she travelled as a singer/dancer moved from one dusty mining camp to the next, stopping wherever there was a faint chance to earn some of the silver and gold the miners dug out of Mother Earth during their backbreaking twelve-hour shifts. As Mae stumbled out of the stage onto the dusty road, she took a look around.

To her surprise, Tombstone was quite large. There were a lot of buildings along the main street, which seemed to accommodate a hell of a lot of saloons.

Well, well, generally money is spent easily where whiskey flows freely out of many barrels.

This year, Tombstone was the place to be. People searching for their lucky strike hoped to find the silver Mother Lode and moved into town in big numbers on a daily basis.

And those men needed distraction from their hard work as much as they needed food and a place to sleep. It was said the saloons in Tombstone were open throughout the full twenty-four hours of the long days, seven days a week.

The carnival group was scheduled to entertain guests at an establishment called the Bird Cage Theatre. Mae thought that was a funny name. However, that house of entertainment had achieved the reputation of being the most notorious honky-tonk in the whole Southwest. It was worth a stop on the group's tour through the frontier areas.

When the show troop checked into a simple boarding house on Fremont Street, they didn't waste any time, but quickly unpacked their trunks and prepared for the first evening at the theater. They were scheduled to meet the owner at the back of the building by sunset. As the carnival group arrived, they could hear the noise of the crowd flowing down the busy street.

"Looks like there's already quite a commotion going on in there," Mae's friend Peter commented. He was an expert trick shooter, and well-liked wherever he had performed so far. Unfortunately, there were always some fools who tried to provoke Peter into a shooting competition, man against man. He was smart enough to avoid any kind of deadly gunfight. It would have thrown the whole carnival knee deep into trouble if Peter left the group, whether due to a bullet or an angry lynch mob. Mae hoped he would be able to avoid trouble here as well, but somehow, she had her doubts. Tombstone's reputation as the town that took a man's life every day had spread far beyond Arizona's borders.

As Peter knocked hard against the wooden door in the rear wall of the theater, Mae was pulled out of her deep reflections about this town. They had to wait for another quarter of an hour until the door opened and a scantily dressed woman stood in front of them. Mae was not surprised at all.

She had seen her share of prostitution all along the frontier and had begun to compare the income of the shady ladies with her own as a circus singer/dancer. It appeared that the soiled doves definitely earned a much higher income than Mae's meager wage.

The lady of the night asked them to follow her to the area behind the stage and sent for Bill Hutchinson, the owner of the house of ill fame. He came around the corner of the heavy stage drapes and greeted them enthusiastically.

"Thank God, you arrived in town just in time. It's payday for the miners, and we have a full house. You can start your show right away!" He hurried off toward the downstairs area of the building.

The group got ready, and Peter entered the stage to start his trick shooting. At the end of Peter's performance, numerous gunshots erupted and Mae, who stood behind the stage drapes, feared for her friend's safety, but Peter came jumping behind the stage, laughing.

"This is the most notorious place I have ever seen. My goodness, it's packed to the limit. They shoot holes in the ceiling instead of cheering. Let's hope they don't put bullet holes into our bellies at the end of our performance. Well, one thing is sure, my children, we can earn a lot of silver here in this dusty town of Tombstone!"

The show went on. At last it was Mae's turn on stage to sing and do her ballet dancing act. She usually sang first since the dance was strenuous and left her with barely any breath for singing. As she entered the stage, she was shocked when she saw the crowd.

The room was packed, and the cigar smoke so thick she couldn't make out the faces in the back near the bar. The upstairs cribs were filled with men and soiled doves. In front of the stage all the tables were occupied with drinking prospectors. They appeared rough and dusty but willing to spend their week's earnings.

Various girls in daring dresses no decent town lady would have ever worn, sat on their laps or moved swiftly from table to table with baskets full of beverages. Some of the girls climbed toward the upstairs cribs with a miners quickly following them.

Mae spoke to the young Irish piano player and asked him to tinkle a well-known tune. At the beginning her voice was barely heard above the noise, but slowly, heads started turning toward the stage. More than one miner's attention was caught by the crystal-clear tone of this beauty.

When Mae turned to the right, she saw him sitting in the first booth next to the stage. He played poker with another man. His hair was long, light brown and wavy, his mustache short and well-trimmed. His gray-blue eyes and high cheek bones added to his handsome features. He didn't pay attention to her, but instead concentrated on the deck of cards in his hand, his face cast in a serious expression. His opponent was a cowboy wearing a red sash, with a pistol holster around his hips. His hair was black. He sat with his back to Mae, and she couldn't see his face. As she finished her song, she earned quite a lot of applause. "So far so good," she mumbled.

One of the carnival group members took the stage with her violin and started playing a Hungarian folksong. Since there were two good looking women on stage now men paid much more attention to what was happening. They expected another song from Mae, but to everyone's surprise she began dancing a daring ballet choreography.

It didn't take long for the prospectors, saddle tramps and gamblers to get on their feet in order to get a better glimpse of the beautiful, extremely flexible woman who could assume positions that fueled every man's fantasies. The audience cheered and clapped enthusiastically.

When the Hungarian song rose from a single violin, Russian Bill looked up. His face conveyed an appreciation and longing for the music of his beloved Russian homeland. Both the woman playing the violin and the beautiful dancer, held his interest. Obviously they were the reasons why men were on their feet pushing and shoving against the edge of the stage.

His friend Curly Bill whom he played poker with every night, had told him about the arrival of a new carnival troop earlier that evening, but Russian Bill had not been interested. His mind was on gambling, and in case he was in need of a woman, he was always welcomed in the more luxurious bordellos around town. A rich, handsome man was never denied anything in the red-light district. The new travelling carnival group held no appeal for him, at least not until now.

The girl on stage whirled around like a dust devil and leaped into a daring classical ballet position.

She turned her face toward his table and flashed him a dazzling smile. Single strands of her dark hair stuck to her sweaty forehead, and her cheeks flamed red from her performance, as she panted hard.

The handsome gambler stared at her breasts held tightly by the costume and saw how they rose and fell while she tried to catch her breath. When she got up and bowed in front of the crowd almost everybody in the theater was clapping. Some of old Bill Clanton's cowboys were shooting at the ceiling which made her jump for a moment. But she waved and smiled at them and quickly ran behind the stage curtain.

"They loved you, darling," Peter exclaimed.

Mae smiled at him. She was tired from travelling to Tombstone and having to perform right away.

Peter told her enthusiastically that they would perform again the following day. Obviously, the owner appreciated their act, and asked them to stay at least two weeks. That meant guaranteed income so they all happily agreed and left the premises to rest after their work and travels.

Meanwhile, on the other side of the stage, Russian Bill watched her leave as he turned the cherry flavored cigar between his fingers. Curly Bill slapped his shoulders, jolting him from his thoughts.

"What's wrong, my Russian prince? Did the little dancing devil impress you so much that you reject your poker game?" A knowing smile showed on Curly Bill's face.

His friend shook his head and returned to his booth. He smiled at Curly Bill for calling him "Russian prince." After all, that was what he was. Well, not exactly a prince but a nobleman indeed, and quite wealthy. He turned his attention back to his deck of cards, but from time to time his thoughts returned to the mysterious dancer on stage.

Who was she?

The next two weeks of performing at the theater passed so quickly, Mae was barely aware of the days. Tombstone had cast its spell on the beautiful young woman, or perhaps a man had cast his spell on her? During the day the dusty streets were busy with thousands of mineworkers, cow hands, storekeepers, and stagecoaches. The air smelled of dust and horse manure.

There was some kind of trouble every day. Triggered by whiskey, opium, or bad luck in gambling, violent fights erupted daily and often came to a deadly end for one of the opponents.

Sometimes a heated discussion about a deck of poker cards or the favors of a painted cat were enough to get a man killed on the busy dusty, streets. Most fights erupted inside the saloons, and many men died in them.

The red-light district was the largest Mae had seen on her travels so far. She had become friends with Lizette, a beautiful girl working at the Bird Cage as the so-called "Flying Nymph." Mae was aware of Lizette's unstable personality but nevertheless liked her a lot. The red-haired sporting girl was the one who suggested Mae leave the carnival and stay behind to earn much better money as an "entertaining lady." Mae still had her difficulties with letting men touch her for money. Well, actually she would not have hesitated if it was one specific man.

By now she knew his name was Russian Bill. At least, that was how he was known in town. She had heard that he claimed to be the son of a Russian noblewoman and must be quite wealthy, as he rented the booth next to the stage every evening. That cost around twenty-five dollars in silver per night, a fortune considering the weekly prospector's pay of five to twelve dollars.

The Handsome European had many friends among a gang of cowboys, and he'd had a couple of heated discussions with the Earp brothers who represented the law in town. Bill saw himself as an outlaw and gambler. But

Mae had difficulties believing that. Behind his hard stare and rough behavior lay a well-educated gentleman with the most astonishing gray-blue eyes she had ever seen. That man lacked the brutal, nasty behavior of such scalawags as the Clanton boys.

It seemed to Mae that nobody believed Bill's story about being a Russian nobleman who had been an elite officer under the ruling Czar. The beautiful dancer had heard people making fun of Bill, and his outlaw buckaroo friends didn't take him seriously as an outlaw.

Mae had watched him playing his card games every night and had to admit that her heart had skipped a beat or two whenever she saw him. Many of the girls were after Russian Bill, and the carnival performer was not foolish enough to risk making enemies with the ladies of the night. However, she had never witnessed him spending the night with one of them, and frankly didn't want to. She had the feeling that it would hurt her more than she cared to admit to anybody, including herself.

CHAPTER 10

***

WHEN THE TWO WEEKS WERE OVER AND THE GROUP WAS ABOUT TO PACK UP
to conquer the next town, Mae told Peter and the others
that she would be staying behind to build a future at the
Bird Cage.

Nobody was surprised, but Peter hugged her hard, asking if she was sure about this. She nodded through tears. He
had been an awesome companion and knew her heart better
than anybody else among the entire group. The trick shooter
had seen the sparks of desire for Russian Bill growing in
his dear friend's eyes and hoped that she would not pay a
high price for listening to her foolish heart. Peter wished her
the very best because he was truly fond of Mae Davenport.

As Mae watched the stagecoach disappearing toward
Benson, she felt a twinge of loneliness in her heart. *Would
she ever see them again?* But it was too late, and she had
made up her mind. Mae still had enough money saved and
would stay in the lodging house for another night or two
until she found a simple home.

Lizette had asked Mae to move in with her and another
girl known as Crazy Anne, who shared a small house, and

Mae seriously considered the possibility. But right now, she felt like being alone for a few days to get used to her new life. She was certain that she would miss the others from the carnival troop.

The bad part about being alone was that she had to face having no company, especially at dinner time. The town's honorable women avoided her in the same way that they bashed every female who worked at the notorious theater. After all, it was no secret that the establishment was more a house of ill repute where gambling, drinking and sinful behavior was available twenty-four hours a day. All performers were outcasts in the eyes of the so-called pure women.

Mae decided to grab a bite at the friendliest place she had been to so far in this ruthless town. It was the small restaurant owned and run by a pretty Irish gal called Nellie Cashman. Actually, Nellie carried the nickname "Angel of the miners' camp," and indeed, she was an angel—friendly and humble and always there for the needy people. Nellie didn't judge anyone and always served meals to the prostitutes. Plus, Mae was pretty convinced that no man would try to get "fresh" with her at Nellie's place. The restaurant owner had earned the equal respect of everybody.

As Mae Davenport walked over to the corner next to a huge water pump which kept the mining shafts dry, she could already smell the mouthwatering aroma of Nellie's cuisine. She sat down and ordered the day's special—meatloaf, fresh potatoes, and homemade lemonade.

Nellie gazed at Mae, and, in her usual straightforward manner, asked about her plans. "So, you're going to stay in Tombstone and are no longer with the carnival, is that right?"

Mae nodded and told her she would continue working at

the Bird Cage. She prepared herself for the expected critical glance or public bashing but it didn't come. Instead, Nellie Cashman sat down at her table and patted her guest's hand.

"I want you to know that the life as a soiled dove is much too dangerous to linger in it for long. Grab as much money as you can, or a decent husband, if you should ever find one in your arms. Please watch out for yourself. Get one of those small guns to hide under your skirts. I want you to know that you are always welcome at one of my tables, Mae Davenport. The frontier is a rough terrain for a woman alone so we ladies need to stick together. Now I need to get your food off the stove. I'll be back." With a smile, she rushed off to the small kitchen at the back of the restaurant. Mae looked around with tears in her eyes.

She was touched by the other woman's humble words. Nellie Cashman had indeed called her a lady. What an astonishing human being she was. Slowly but surely Mae understood why Nellie was called the Angel of the camp.

"She's a great person, isn't she?" A low voice with a foreign accent and a soft timbre next to her made her jump. Russian Bill stood right beside her table. She had not seen him approach, and now here he was, his head slightly bowed in greeting. Mae had never spoken to him before. The impact of hearing his voice was astonishing. He touched the second chair.

"May I?" he asked.

The dark-haired woman nodded slowly, still too surprised about meeting him here and slightly annoyed with herself that her cheeks felt flushed and hot.

"May I introduce myself officially? I am William Tattenbaum, but everyone calls me Russian Bill. And you are?"

Finally, she found her voice again and answered with

a shy smile. "Mae Davenport, known as Mae Davenport."

He smiled about her obvious sense of humor. "Actually, you are wrong about that, Miss Davenport. At the Bird Cage you are already known as the "Dancing Fawn.""

She stared at him, cheeks even redder. "Are you teasing, sir?"

"Call me Bill, please, and it is true. They call you a dancing fawn due to your huge dark eyes and, forgive me for being so blunt, also due to your shapely legs, which are exposed for everyone's pleasure each time you dance. No reason to feel ashamed, Mae Davenport. You are indeed a beauty."

The sound of his voice made her shiver. Hearing it felt like a tender touch.

Mae was glad to see Nellie walking over with a plate of steaming food because she felt as if she might faint at any minute. This man honestly confused her. He was a gambler, perhaps an outlaw, yet he spoke with the highest manners and dignity. William Tattenbaum obviously was an educated man. Maybe the rumors about him being a nobleman were not false after all.

Nellie looked at Bill. "Howdy, Bill. Did you drop your cards for the sake of one of my decent lunches?"

"Actually, it is so, indeed, Miss Nellie. You know I cannot resist your meatloaf. It is much too delicious."

"So, I reckon I will bring you a plate full of it. Where will you sit?" she asked with a broad smile.

The good-looking gambler glanced at Mae, a trace of unexpected uncertainty showing on his handsome features. Mae said, "You can eat at my table, of course. I don't fancy eating alone, anyway."

"Very well then," said Nellie and returned to her kitchen.

"Thank you, Miss Davenport."

"Call me Mae, please."

"Of course, then Mae it will be." He studied her face for a moment. When he spoke again, he looked a bit concerned. "I heard you decided to stay here to continue performing at the Bird Cage. Is that true?"

"Looks like news travels fast in this town," she answered with a broad grin.

The gambler nodded. "That is true. I hope you are aware that you are going to encounter dangerous situations in the future. The life of a fallen angel can be prosperous, yet deadly, too, Mae."

She blushed again and put down her fork. She was clearly embarrassed. He obviously knew right away that her new performing arrangement did not only include dancing and singing.

"Please, don't misunderstand me, my dear. I accept your decision. This is your life; who am I to judge you? I am a gambler. I want you to be aware of the dangers. I also want you to know that you can count on me as a friend if you should ever need any help."

The carnival performer was completely taken by surprise and asked him bluntly how she deserved such an offer after he heard what she was going to soon become. William Tattenbaum looked deeply into her eyes. *A man could lose his soul in those eyes.* She touched his senses in more than one way, but she didn't yet know it.

"Mae, I come from a country far away and often miss it. I feel homesick, you could say. But for reasons I want to keep to myself I cannot return. Your music and dance send me back to my home soil when I watch you perform. It warms my heart, and I'm less lonely. It almost feels as if my family is around me, but I will most likely never see them again. As a matter of fact, I feel close to them when I hear you sing and watch you doing the Hungarian gypsy dance. You know, it's true that one can find a home in another person."

The astonished singer was speechless. That was likely the most beautiful thing anyone had ever told her about her performance, and it touched her heart deeply. She knew the dark hours of loneliness far too well. Mae Davenport also had to leave her family behind. Her parents and siblings had banned her from their fancy home where she grew up on the East Coast. When her family discovered she wanted to become a singer and dancer, they had tried to shatter her dreams and wishes for independence by planning to marry her to an old business partner of her father's. When she refused to do so, they had locked her in her room for weeks, until one day she managed to escape, knowing she would never see her family again. It broke her heart, but the call of freedom had been too strong to resist.

Russian Bill touched her elbow gently. She shook off the unpleasant thoughts of the past and looked at him. A silent understanding passed between them that told each they had constantly battled the same ghosts of their past.

They ate their meal in silence, but it was not unpleasant. When Nellie came to clear the table, the handsome gambler gave her enough coins for both meals. He hushed Mae's protest with a single fingertip to his lips. "It was a true pleasure for me, Mae, so paying for your meal is the least I can do."

Mae returned to the theater the same evening. She felt awkward being there without her troop of carnival performers, but faced it as bravely as possible. William Tattenbaum sat in his booth as usual, handing out a deck of cards to one of the cowboy friends of Curly Bill, and greeted her warmly. She smiled at him and walked on stage to get ready for her first song.

CHAPTER 11

***

SOMEONE GENTLY SLAPPED HER FACE.

"Hey there, wake up, will you!"

Cheryl slowly opened her eyes and looked straight into Heather's face. Things were still blurry and she didn't know where she was. Slowly, she turned her head. A small bump had started to form on her forehead, which hurt when touched. A severe headache. Must have hit the banister at the small stairs next to the stage. As she tried to stand, Heather helped her to her feet.

"What happened, girl?"

Cheryl shook her head, confused. "I have no idea. I wanted to walk behind the stage but I fell and I don't remember anything after that."

"Let's go to the front. I have some water. Tell you what, you keep the ticket and finish your tour another day when you feel better. Maybe you're not used to the altitude here."

Cheryl looked at Heather. It seemed as if the museum employee was nervous, or wanted to get rid of her. She waited a little while, drinking some of the offered water in the foyer. When Cheryl felt better, she agreed to come by on her next day off to explore the rest of the artifacts with her purchased ticket.

At home, the confused woman had brewed some coffee but the mug sat on the small table next to her, untouched.

What's happening to me? Second time to faint within a few days. Weird that I've felt fine before each time. Am I getting sick? Should I get a checkup at the hospital? I'll ask Dorothea to recommend a good doctor and help with getting me an appointment.

Closing her eyes, she touched the mug absently. Her thoughts returned to the Bird Cage. She had never been there before that day, but the place seemed so familiar to her. It was truly bewildering. And weird that she had felt at peace there, as if she knew every part of the building well.

She shook her head at this thought. Cheryl smelled the rich flavor of the coffee, yet there was another scent that still lingered in her nose as well. It was the smooth aroma of cherry cigars. What in the world was happening to her?

The next few days Cheryl worked at the Courthouse Museum but seemed to be preoccupied from time to time as she reviewed the weird visit at the historic theater, feeling foolish at the same time for doing so. Dorothea started to get concerned and asked Cheryl if everything was alright.

"Everything is just fine. I think the long hours of studying in the evenings are starting to take their toll."

But her superior's face showed a knowing expression.

"Remember when I said that Tombstone has a way of sharing its history with a small number of people in a very special way?"

Cheryl waited without answering but recalled the conversation. Dorothea's face bore a serious expression. "It seems you are one of those rare people to whom Tombstone really speaks."

"What do you mean? I don't get it."

Her elder friend gently rotated the glass she held between her fingers, 'round and 'round, trying to find the right words. "I know this may sound nutty or just plain silly, but some people, including me by the way, see things in Tombstone that cannot be explained by science or books. There are haunted areas here, and the Bird Cage is known to be a hotspot for such activities."

Cheryl laughed out loud. "Wait a minute. Are you saying there are ghosts in Tombstone, and that you've actually seen them yourself?"

"Sure sounds crazy, but I know what I've seen since we moved here."

"I don't know what to say. You're talking ghosts and spirits."

There was that voice on the porch. No one was around. And the smell of cherry cigars. Again, no one around. Was it really possible? Restless souls from the Old West haunting this place?

Dorothea touched her hand. "Take your time to think about this. Whenever you're ready, I'll tell you what I've experienced since we have been living here. I can assure you that I know my great-grandmother pretty well by now."

The museum manager continued with her chores while Cheryl remained seated for a moment.

Maybe they're playing a trick on me. New girl and all that. Ghosts? How silly. Yet a tiny flame of curiosity had started to lick at Cheryl's subconscious.

Her next off day was a sunny Wednesday, beautiful with crisp, cool air. *Maybe another trip to the Bird Cage? Use my ticket to explore the rest of the building? Or stay away from that place?*

Drinking a strong cup of the Arbuckle coffee that Bert

had gotten her hooked on, she watched two cardinals hopping from one branch of the rose bush to another. Cheryl decided she was much too curious to let the opportunity slip by so she dressed in jeans and a white blouse, and walked briskly to the upper part of the tourist area and straight to the old Adobe structure.

Heather wasn't there and Cheryl was relieved, embarrassed by what had happened during her last visit. She had never liked being the center of attention.

The attractive woman explained who she was to the lady behind the entrance counter. "I wasn't able to finish the tour on my last visit."

"Oh, you're the gal working at the courthouse, right? Heather told me to let you in for free if you came by."

"Thanks so much." *I wonder if Heather told her I kind of fainted.*

"Feel free to come back to the front room if you have any questions after strolling through the entire place. Otherwise, the tour leads through the gift store to the side exit next to the parking lot," the lady said, then opened the door to the main theater for her.

Cheryl walked into the dark room, cautiously taking each step. The cribs on the second floor stared down like the cold eyes of a stranger. Her skin immediately developed goosebumps after setting foot into the main room.

I won't touch the piano this time.

She walked quickly by the poker booth, and hurriedly climbed the small stairs entering the section behind the curtain. On an impulse, she turned her head and looked back. "I thought smoking is prohibited in the entire building" she mumbled while she stared at the swirls of cigar smoke curling against the ceiling of the booth next to the stage.

Where did that smoke come from? And I can't remember the deck of cards with the queen of hearts next to the bottle. Was it there on my last visit?

Somehow standing behind the stage curtain made Cheryl happy. She didn't know why but she felt like stepping onto the stage to dance and sing. Joy swept through her. At least, until she turned around and looked straight at the black- and gold-colored hearse standing in the far corner about twenty feet behind the stage.

By now she had heard people talk about the "Black Moriah," the hearse for the last journey of the dead to Tombstone's Boot Hill. Yet standing next to it was a different story. It made her skin crawl with fear. She could sense the dead who had been transported within it. Cheryl knew instantly that this was not one of the many Tombstone movie props that were displayed throughout the entire town. No, this was the real deal. Dead people of the notorious past had travelled in this piece of ghostly, yet beautifully crafted machinery trimmed with real Tombstone silver and sheet gold.

A small child's coffin leaned against the wheel of the hearse and nearly brought Cheryl to tears. She shivered and wanted to leave, right now! The frightened woman didn't want to picture a small, innocent child resting on the faded linen inside the tiny wooden coffin. She could hardly stand the thought of a mother weeping over that casket and thought she should return to the main entrance to leave.

"Mae, come to me, please!"

There it was again, the soothing low voice she had heard days before. Cheryl turned toward the sound of it.

"Mae, I am waiting for you. Come to me!"

She was not aware of setting one foot in front of the other, slowly walking toward another staircase at the rear wall leading downstairs into the building's basement and further into the past of the Bird Cage Theatre.

With each step she drew closer to the strong smell of the cigar. She heard the clinking of whiskey glasses and the jingle of coins being thrown on top of each other among the shuffling sound of poker cards—familiar sounds to her ears. Her heart pounded loudly as she reached the bottom of the stairs.

There was a small bar and a poker table full of chips, coins, and old faded playing cards. A smaller table sat against the rear wall. Next to it Cheryl saw a cellar behind metal bars brown with corrosion. It looked like a mining shaft full of old whiskey barrels, ladders, and such. That vault-shaped cellar looked rather messy, resembling an antique junk yard.

Cheryl turned toward the three wooden doors to her right opposite the gambling area. They were closed, but the museum owners had removed a board in the middle of the first two doors so one could glance into the sparsely lit, small rooms. Cheryl gasped at the sight.

Inside the first room stood a bed, a small, antique armoire, and a nightstand holding a petroleum lamp next to a cheval mirror. The wallpaper sported a faded flower design that most likely had been a rich red during its best days. But now it had turned into stain-battered brown that peeled from the walls in more than one spot. An antique stove stood in a corner near the mirror. The threadbare mat at the foot of the bed had faded and showed holes.

Cheryl looked into the room, and felt a powerful sensation of emotional pain. There was a small sign next to the door explaining to visitors that this was one of the original prostitution rooms of the higher priced calico queens.

Cheryl kept staring into the tiny chamber, imagining

how women followed their trade in here while men on the other side of the door gambled at the poker table. Whoever sat there must have been aware of the events on the other side of the wooden wall. Everybody down here would have seen the men entering those rooms with the soiled doves. *Did they pay attention or were they too hypnotized by the poker cards and the stack of money and silver on the table?*

She felt a pang of grief as she imagined the abuse those women must have faced and glanced at the dusty cheval mirror. It had gone half blind with age. Its carved wooden frame holding the glass was a beautiful example of antique craftsmanship.

Cheryl looked into that very mirror through the opening in the door and saw her face reflecting blurrily. But strangely the face did not resemble hers. A dark-haired woman with huge eyes looked back at her, a sad smile on her face.

The museum's visitor was too shocked to move. She blinked a couple of times, hoping her eyes only played a trick on her in the semidarkness of the basement. When she opened them again, the woman was still there and raised her hand, motioning Cheryl to come in.

CHAPTER 12

★★★

MAE KNEW IF SHE WANTED TO MAKE GOOD MONEY AND CONTINUE TO WORK AT the Bird Cage there was no way out. She had to offer herself to the men who paid for her company. Fortunately, she was considered for the downstairs bordello rooms and not the cheap cribs above the main theater.

Down here in the basement was where the big money rolled. It was the place where the gents who were better off would seek services of personal pleasures from her. But Mae also knew that those kinds of men had the tendency to ask for more exotic kinds of pleasure due to the higher amount of money they paid, sometimes even brutal favors.

The poker game was rolling for months now and had never been interrupted. Lizette had told her that it cost well over a thousand dollars to buy yourself into it as a player, not that there was often a chair available.

"A thousand dollars!" Mae couldn't believe it. Lizette nodded her head eagerly.

"Yes, my dear, there's big money in Tombstone and believe it or not, so far they have not found the motherlode of silver. If you handle them men down here smartly, they will pay you a fortune. And you, with your looks and dance skills, can ask for almost any price.

"What's even better, my dear, you do not have to give your favors to every dirty prospector that walks into this establishment. You can select when you're working down here at the basement rooms. It is you who decides who gets to lay with you. Of course, Hutchinson keeps half of the price for the house. But you will still earn more than enough."

"It seems that you really enjoy working here, Lizette. To be honest, I am not so convinced that I will ever be able to feel comfortable like you do about offering myself to strangers. But at least I am willing to give it a try, and to see so much kelter on the table is indeed a tempting sight. However, I have no intention to live the life of a calico queen for too long. Once I made enough money, I will seek a better future for myself."

Lizette and Crazy Anne taught Mae all the tricks. From getting guests drunk so they could not perform their male needs anymore to staying sober themselves by hiding bottles of tea the color of whiskey behind the bar. The bartenders worked hand-in-hand with the soiled doves. Her new friends showed her how to emphasize the beauty of her face by coloring her cheeks and her lips with the juice of raspberries or where to place perfumed pieces of linen to keep the stench of sweat and cigars away from her skin.

It did not take long before Mae Davenport was a well sought-after lady of the night at the house of ill repute and was indeed able to select her paying customers. They paid in pure silver coins, and the former carnival singer had gathered a small fortune already.

The only thing that bothered her was what Russian Bill might be thinking of her. They had not spoken since their meal at Nellie Cashman's restaurant. They greeted each other from across the room, but that was it. Somehow his opinion of her mattered a great deal.

A week later Mae decided to wear the shiny, red bustle dress she had sewn with the help of Crazy Anne. Mae looked absolutely gorgeous in it with her petite figure. She had moved into Lizette's and Crazy Anne's house. The three girls shared the costs and had made the place a home where they spent their daytime chatting away happily, cooking, and sewing their own wardrobe. A decent, respected seamstress would not have been willing to be at their service at any time.

They were loved by the men in town yet hated by the so-called pure ladies of the community. The town's "decent" women who gossiped so nastily about the sporting girls at the most famous brothel in Tombstone would have been surprised at how often their beloved husbands spent their time in the arms of the fallen angels. Funny enough though despite all the bashing against the prostitutes, their money was never rejected when donated to the local church or other institutions of the town. Mae had a strong dislike for hypocrites so she stayed away from the female population of Tombstone, unless they were painted cats like her.

So that specific evening Mae arrived at the Bird Cage looking stunning in the red outfit. Mister Hutchinson pulled her aside as soon as she walked behind the stage.

"I have a special guest for you tonight, Mae. He paid in advance for the whole night. You get a share of forty dollars in silver." The beautiful woman stared at the owner of the most notorious place in the West.

That was a small fortune, and Mae wondered who was willing to pay such an amount and even a bigger share to Hutchinson to spend an entire night with her. She went downstairs and straight to the first crib next to the poker area and waited for her lover of the night behind the closed door. She hoped that the man did not have any brutal preferences when it came to the physical favors he had paid for. A few days ago, one of the girls had been brutally raped and her face had been cut with a Bowie knife. With her visage destroyed, only making a living in the shabby cribs on Sixth Street was left for the unfortunate girl. The incident had shaken up all of them and reminded Mae to never forget the dangers of her new life. She had followed Nellie Cashman's advice and had bought a small Derringer which was well hidden under her skirts.

She closed the door but still heard the poker game going on with its background sounds of hollering and male cursing and the faint laughter of the girl in the room next door.

Mae poked at the fire burning in the small stove. It had cooled down in the building and she was thankful for the warm glow of embers. She hoped that her customer took care of his body. Although a prostitute, now she hated bad-smelling men, and often the stench of whiskey and beer together with old sweat was overwhelming upstairs, especially the closer one got to the main bar.

She lowered the light of the petroleum lamp and watched her own shadow dance across the wall. As Mae studied the wallpaper with its flowery design, she heard the door opening behind her.

A wave of piano music and loud laughter drifted into the room, which indicated that her lover for the night had entered. Mae was about to turn as a whispering voice asked her to remain standing still with her back to him.

He spoke softly, and she could barely understand what he said but she felt him moving closer. The man softly touched both of her shoulders. Mae felt his chest leaning against her back and was nervous. She wanted to see who he was but the unknown feller would not allow her to turn. He held her tight and Mae was getting worried. Then he kissed her neck. It was a gentle caress, and she could not help but enjoy it.

His hands moved from her shoulders down, following her spine to her waist where they rested a moment. Slowly, without hurry, he unlaced her corset. She held her breath as he slid it from her slender torso.

Mae had never been undressed with such tenderness. His hands traced every inch of her bare skin and it left her shivering with arousal. She heard a pocket watch being laid onto the small nightstand and the sound of fabric falling on the ground.

The next thing she felt was a bare, warm chest being pressed against her back while he cradled her into his embrace. Skin to skin they stood, soaking up each other's warmth. His chest felt muscular, his stomach flat. The musky scent of his naked torso added to her excitement.

"Turn around, Mae," he instructed.

Surprised, the dark-haired woman stared wide-eyed into the handsome features of Russian Bill and she immediately felt like covering herself, but he shook his head. "Don't feel ashamed, Mae."

"How am I supposed to feel? You paid so go ahead and take what the price is for." She did not mean to hurt him but was too shocked to learn that he was the one who had paid for a full night with her. Of all the men in this house of sin Mae Davenport had never wanted him to buy her body. She was behaving ridiculously, and knew it as she was nothing but a servant of sin but could not help it. Shame and grief flushed through her, causing her eyes to burn with tears.

He looked hurt as he picked up his shirt and vest. "You can keep the money. I do not need to force myself onto a woman, Mae Davenport. Generally, they are far more welcoming than you are."

She felt as if he had slapped her across the face. He was getting dressed and was about to walk out the door, barely able to control his anger and disappointment. Grabbing the door knob, he stood still when she called him back.

"Of all the men in this place, you are the only one I am worried about what you may think of me. Who can respect a woman like me? You know what I earn my money with, especially now since I work here without the carnival group. Why pay that high price, why book me for the entire night? Is your hunger for a woman so endless?"

She shivered and held onto her dress. But strangely she did not want him to leave.

Mae was deeply confused, not knowing how to handle these unknown emotions crashing over her like a cold wave. She felt like a fool and ashamed to the bone.

He turned slowly. "I did it because I wanted to be with you the whole night. You, and not just any woman, Mae. I did buy you the entire night because I can't stand the thought of someone else laying hands on you after I share this bed with you. The reason why I paid is because I could not hold back my passion and desire for you any longer, but I was obviously wrong, because I thought you felt the same way."

"I do, Bill, but as a woman and not as a soiled dove. I want the same but not for the silver, rather for the sake of feeling you and to touch your heart and soul as much as that body of yours. Yes, I desire you but you see me as the sporting woman I am because you paid to lay hands on me and never showed that you felt anything for me at all."

She spun, feeling devastated. *This was going wrong; he should not be here; she should not be here.* Her eyes were moist. He looked back at her, and walked over to where she stood like an insecure child with tears streaming down her flushed cheeks. Bill was drawn to her like a moth to a flame. As he raised her chin with his fingers, he forced her to look into his eyes that had turned smoky dark gray with desire. Russian Bill was glaring down at her, a demanding expression on his face.

"Then prove to me that you want me, Mae. Let me feel it!"

He didn't wait for her to answer but kissed her, hard and passionately, and Mae returned that kiss with a hunger previously unknown to her. She was swept away by the intensity of it, and the way her body reacted to his.

The Bird Cage Theatre and the poker game outside vanished in a storm of passion and lust that raged behind the door of the first chamber. Neither held anything back. They surrendered to their feelings which they had controlled for much too long. The two lovers conquered each other's body, explored every inch of skin, and bathed in each other's passion for hours.

They drowned in each other's lust, not willing to give in to physical exhaustion. The night was still young, and Russian Bill bought Mae until dawn with the shine of the silver dollars he had placed in Hutchinson's hands. He would make her his for that night and hopefully for good.

CHAPTER 13

* * *

CHERYL STARED BACK AT THE IMAGE IN THE DUSTY MIRROR. A LIGHT FLAVOR of cherry cigars hung in the air. She touched her lips.

There was a whispering voice. "Do you feel me Mae? I missed you so."

As Cheryl turned around to follow the sound of the voice, she looked back at the small cellar with its dirt floor next to the third crib. The door of the third chamber was closed. No board had been removed. It was not possible to glance into that room. Nevertheless, Cheryl walked toward it. A small sign announced it would be opening soon for public viewing, and it had been the bathroom and changing room for the gamblers.

Cheryl walked closer and carefully touched the door. It felt cold, and she was overwhelmed with the sudden stench of decaying flesh seeping through the wood. She stumbled backwards and bumped against the banister in front of the gambling area.

"Mae, stay away! I cannot protect you if you enter there," the voice echoed in her head, a whisper with a threatening tone.

Cheryl quickly walked away from the bar area, almost stumbling into the next room of the museum. The stench nearly made her gag but the farther her feet led her from the basement chambers, the sadder she felt as well. For some reason she did not want to leave.

The adjoining room displayed many old photos and documents such as prostitute licenses that permitted the ladies of the line to offer their services in the world's oldest trade. To her surprise there was even one framed at the rear wall for Mae Davenport.

A single tear rolled over Cheryl's cheek. She knew she was somehow connected to the destiny of Mae, but did not understand how and why.

"Good heavens, what in the world was that terrible smell?" she mumbled, still feeling nauseous. Cheryl walked back to the main entrance. The lady there smiled at her.

"Did you enjoy your tour? Any questions?"

"Have you ever heard of a woman called Mae Davenport?" Cheryl asked.

"Hmmm, let me think. Oh yes, now I remember. She came to Tombstone during its silver boom time, like most of the girls, of course. Mae was the member of a carnival group but stayed behind when the troop left for another boomtown, if I recall correctly. She continued to work as a soiled dove or prostitute, as you would call them today. We have her license issued by the town's marshal of that time. And guess what, it was indeed the famous Virgil Earp who signed that very license. The town made lots of money with the women of loose morals. Each lady of the night had to pay a fee to the city or she wouldn't have been allowed to offer her services. The town council had them examined by the doctor at least once a month to avoid spreading disease. Much smarter than nowadays if you ask me."

Cheryl was fascinated. "So, the townsfolk treated the calico queens like outcasts but accepted their money nevertheless, although it was earned in sin."

The lady nodded eagerly. "Yes indeed, that's the way it was. By the way, I'm Teresa. I'm sorry I was so busy opening this place up this morning and I didn't even introduce myself."

The other woman took her outstretched hand. "Cheryl. Pleasure to meet you, Teresa."

The lady behind the old bar looked thoughtful for a moment. "You know, not all folks in town disliked the shady ladies. The men, the miners, of course loved them.

"It was hard work to dig for silver and many died much too young. Some drowned in the flooded mines because the deeper they dug, the higher the ground-water level rose. Some lost their lives in collapsing shafts, and many of them passed away because of consumption—tuberculosis—like our famous Doc Holliday. A lot of prospectors got killed by syphilis and gave that disease to many working girls as well. All these men were so thankful for the female attention they got, so they didn't mind having to pay for it. In my opinion the fallen angels indeed built up the frontier and conquered the West at least as much as all the miners, cowboys, and gunfighters did, if not more."

"Sounds as if you are actually very fond of them, Teresa." Cheryl looked at the older women who was dressed in a romantic mint green Victorian bustle dress with a matching hat. She looked so authentic she could have stepped right out of an 1882 Western scene.

Teresa patted Cheryl's hand. "You've only been here a few weeks. You'll understand soon, believe me. You're right, I am very fond of the ladies of the night. I studied a lot about them. So did your boss, Dorothea, by the way.

Some of the women were tragic personalities. Some of them so unhappy they committed suicide. Many were alcoholics and laudanum addicts, but believe me, if their help was needed, they always stood by the needy ones. Some of the madams running brothels opened their places during times of disease and took care of the sick. They converted their houses of ill fame into hospitals and pampered many sick miners back to life without charging them."

Teresa laughed at Cheryl's surprised facial expression. "Not the kind of behavior one would expect when talking of prostitutes, right? But it's the truth. The museum even has historical paperwork proving it."

Cheryl nodded. Then she shook Teresa's hand again. "Thank you for your patience and explanations, Teresa. I hope to chat with you another time. But there's a group of tourists walking over, so I don't want to keep you from work any longer."

"You're always welcome, sweetie. Come and visit me again. Check my working hours with Heather. It's great to meet someone who's genuinely interested in the history here."

Cheryl was about to walk out the door but suddenly remembered and turned around again. "Teresa, I almost forgot! Down there in the area of the third door opposite the small bar, it smells really bad like a dead animal rotting away or something."

The lady behind the counter hesitated. "Must be a critter or a stray cat. Most likely it snuck in during the day and couldn't find a way out. Happens from time to time. Well, it won't smell for long. Everything is so dry here, it'll mummify pretty fast."

Cheryl doubted that explanation. "If it's in the third room, I think it would be easier to remove it before the smell gets too bad."

But the museum employee shook her head looking worried, almost scared. "Girl, none of us ever enters the third room. It's not safe." She quickly turned away and pretended to count her change while she waited for the tourists who were slowly strolling toward the door, debating whether they should spend the money on the admission fee or not.

There was no chance to ask Teresa what she had meant about the room not being safe as the eager employee had already started greeting the tourists.

Cheryl turned and left. She didn't see the worried expression on Teresa's face.

On the way back to her temporary home, Cheryl bought two books at a local bookstore. "Soiled Doves of the West" and "Tombstone's Red-Light District." She planned to spend the rest of the day reading and enjoying her time off.

As soon as she arrived home, Cheryl started her beloved coffee maker and prepared herself some pasta. Not the typical Western cuisine for her, but spaghetti with meat sauce was her personal soul food.

Soon the house was filled with mouthwatering aromas and Cheryl fixed herself a plate of the tasty Italian meal. She always took pride in her talents as a cook. While eating alone at the kitchen table, her thoughts returned to the historical theater and to the face she had seen in that Cheval mirror of the downstairs crib. *Did that really happen, or is my imagination going wild with all this weird stuff?*

Her modern education forbade her to believe any of this was real, but somehow in a corner of her mind she knew there was more to it.

The voice she'd been hearing on and off sounded so familiar and comforting. The smell of the cherry cigars was a welcomed flavor although she didn't smoke at all.

When she finished her meal, she poured herself some coffee, sat on the porch, and opened the first book, "Red-Light District of Tombstone" by Ben Traywick. According to the information at the back of the book he was a historian and still lived in Tombstone.

Cheryl read the first few lines and was hooked on the book right away. Her coffee sat on the small table next to her rocking chair, forgotten, like the traffic moving up and down the street from time to time.

She barely looked up when a car or motorcycle drove by and even forgot to wave at the stagecoach team rattling along the street on their way home.

Her reading was only interrupted once for a necessary stop at the bathroom and to grab her warm shawl. With one foot folded under her lap, the student continued. The book was about the hardships, and the money made in the red-light district which originally covered an unbelievable six blocks of old Tombstone. Cheryl looked at the pictures of the women printed in the paperback book, and touched their cheeks gently.

When she flipped a page, Lizette's face stared back at her from a haunting, sepia-colored image. The soiled dove looked fragile yet gorgeous with long wavy hair which appeared to be a fiery copper tone in the portrait.

Cheryl stared at the picture. She was not even aware of her own tears. The only emotion she felt was the shock of recognizing Lizette. *But how was that possible?* That fallen angel had lived over a hundred years ago, yet she knew her. Cheryl sobbed as she read about Lizette's success as the "Flying Nymph" at the Bird Cage, and her devastating self-destruction caused by a life ruled by alcoholism and mental issues. Lizette had ended it tragically by committing suicide.

When Cheryl stopped reading, she had reached the last page of the book and it was getting dark. *Oh, my Goodness, it is evening already. I didn't feel the time passing by,* she had been so captivated by the paperback.

She looked again at the pictures of Mae Davenport, and of Lizette whose family name remained a secret hidden in the past. Her whole Tombstone adventure felt like a dream, and for the first time in her life the modern days with its cars, mobile phones, and computers appeared unreal and strange to her.

Cheryl walked into the house and stared at the TV in the tiny living room. It sat there on the sideboard like an unwanted intruder on top of the beautifully crafted furniture. The electronic device didn't fit in at all. She didn't bother to turn it on but instead showered and went straight to bed, switching her phone off. She felt exhausted.

Her dreams were filled with images of a crowded saloon and a beautiful Lizette swinging above the audience on a thin cable made of steel. The "Flying Nymph" smiled at Cheryl in her dreams and she smiled back.

CHAPTER 14

***

THE NEXT DAY DOROTHEA INVITED CHERYL TO HAVE DINNER WITH HER RIGHT
after work. The young woman asked her boss about Mae
Davenport, and the manager of the courthouse shared
what she knew.

"She came to town with a carnival group but stayed
in Tombstone as a woman of ill fame. She could make
much more money in that trade. Rumor had it that she was
seriously involved with a gambler at the Bird Cage by the
name of Russian Bill. He was another tragic figure of the
silver boom and claimed to be the son of a noblewoman
in Russia. That's how he got his nickname. Fact is, he
died under tragic circumstances. Wanted so much to be an
outlaw, and in the end, I think he was hanged. Mae was
said to have been madly in love with him and never got
over losing the love of her life."

The waitress of The Depot restaurant brought their piz-
za. As they started to eat, Cheryl asked her friend where
she had gotten all the information. Dorothea hesitated for a
moment. When she spoke, her cheeks blushed. "Most of it
from doing research in old town papers. When we took over

the courthouse, we found a whole bunch of old documents in the attic. But Crazy Anne told me some."

"Who is Crazy Anne?" Cheryl waited for the answer and stopped chewing for a moment. Dorothea shrugged her shoulders.

"As a matter of fact, Crazy Anne is my great-grand-mother, the one who owned the house you're staying in."

Cheryl still didn't get it. "So, you must have found a diary or something like that. How awesome."

But the woman sitting opposite shook her head. "No Cheryl, she speaks to me about these things."

Cheryl stared and didn't know what to say. An embarrassing silence developed between them. Dorothea raised her hands as if to apologize.

"I know this is hard to believe, and I don't expect you to. You asked me a straight question and I answered it honestly. I have seen Crazy Anne more than once and, believe me, at the beginning I doubted my own sanity. When I saw her the first time, I bought a new pair of glasses thinking maybe there was something wrong with my eyes. After a few appearances she started to talk to me. She told me things about the old days which the documents I mentioned later confirmed. The people she named, the trials that took place, it's all there in those records. Prostitutes and performers of the Bird Cage she told me about, they all really existed. There were details you can't find in the tourist books or souvenir shops. Believe me, it scared the wits out of me in the beginning. When I told Bert about it, he was about to sign me up for a loony bin. But then, one day he saw her, too. That was when we got knee-deep in research. Everything she told me proved to be true."

Cheryl shook her head. She liked the McEntires a lot and somehow, she knew the woman was not making up the story. Yet she could not bring herself to believe all this. She had been brought up in a world of science and modern education.

This whole town seemed stuck in the 1880s in more ways than one. And it seemed Tombstone changed the people living here.

The rest of the evening passed with shallow small talk. Both women were glad when the waitress came with their check. After paying and putting on their jackets, they walked to Dorothea's truck but Cheryl told her she would rather walk home. Dorothea hesitated a moment but then wished her a good night.

"Okay, Cheryl, see you tomorrow at the courthouse. Thanks for joining me for dinner."

The California student waved goodbye and watched the pickup's rear lights disappear around the corner. She walked slowly along the quiet street, lost in thought about what her friend had told her about Crazy Anne.

A sudden cold breeze across her cheeks made her raise her gaze, wondering where the chilly wind came from. She stood in front of the Bird Cage. She had not paid attention to where she was after leaving the restaurant.

The old structure looked different at night. It seemed to want to entrap her like an enemy. She felt a tugging sensation toward the building, and goosebumps started to show on her arms. Out of nowhere a menacing voice called her.

"You're supposed to get to work. Come on over here. You're late." The voice wasn't the one she had heard before. It was more like a growl. She walked toward the main entrance with its brown double doors, not aware of where her steps took her.

"Do not make me come for you. Get to work right now!" The cold breeze was all around Cheryl now and she feared the source of the voice. She heard it loud and clear. As she was about to touch the front door the sudden aroma of the cherry cigar smoke enfolded her.

"Mae, my love, you must leave! He is evil and will not let you go if you step through the entrance now." The pleasant voice she knew so well was an urgent whisper close to her right ear.

She felt someone standing next to her but couldn't see a soul on the street. She turned around and followed the aroma of the cigar smoke that led her further down Allen Street and away from the old museum. All she knew was that she could trust the voice leading her. Cheryl walked as if in a trance, and suddenly she stood in front of her guest house.

"Mae, you can never enter the Bird Cage at night unless you are with me."

Cheryl shook her head. "My name is Cheryl. I don't know who you are and why, for Christ's sake, don't you show yourself to me, you coward!"

There was a moment of silence and she turned to unlock her door. "That may be your name now, but your real name is Mae, Mae Davenport." As the words vanished into the night Cheryl stared into the darkness. The smell of the cigars was gone.

The perplexed woman was frustrated and deeply bothered by the outcome of the evening. What had happened in front of that old brothel? The man she had heard sounded rude, angry, and somehow dangerous. And then there was that second voice which she had heard a couple of times before. So kind and soothing. Its sound tugged at some part of her subconscious. *I know that voice from somewhere, but every time I think I remember it slips my mind again. I seem to know that man but I cannot make a connection. Who is he?*

Cheryl was also deeply disturbed by the way the evening with Dorothea had gone at the restaurant and was afraid she might have been unkind to her superior, who had also become a dear friend by now. "I have to apologize tomorrow," Cheryl said into the empty room. *After all, who am I to judge other people's beliefs?*

She went to bed still upset and tossed and turned in the throes of a nightmare where she was in a smoky room. The stage was filled with can-can dancers, and the men were on their feet. But Cheryl was on the way downstairs where she knew the stranger who spoke so tenderly to her would be waiting. In her dream she opened the door to the first room where he turned and smiled at her. She saw his face in her dreams. His wavy, long hair framed his handsome features. His blue-grayish eyes looked at her with a warmth that sent shivers down her spine, and his sensual lips were curled into a welcoming smile as he held out a hand. She rushed into his arms and whispered, "Bill, my beloved Russian Bill."

CHAPTER 15

***

CHERYL AWOKE WITH A SPLITTING HEADACHE. SHE BREWED HER COFFEE stronger than usual and swallowed two aspirin, hoping they would work quickly. Tired, she closed her bloodshot eyes and rubbed her temples. Immediately, Cheryl saw the face from her dreams before her inner eye and felt a warm tingle in her belly.

My God, get yourself together woman. It's ridiculous that you're dreaming of an outlaw from the 1880s and having the hots for him. Good gracious, you must miss civilization too much. However much she scolded herself, the events and dreams of last evening didn't vanish and they caused her to smile.

When she met Dorothea at work, she had made up her mind to talk openly with her. Dorothea greeted her warmly but hesitated to start a conversation. Before Cheryl could talk to her, the sheriff walked into the museum, greeting them with a tip to his cowboy hat.

"Good morning, ladies. I came to inform you that we have called off the search for Lisa. It looks like she ran away from town. And even if she didn't, this is going to be a cold case nevertheless, until new evidence pops up. Just wanted to let you know. But remember, if you come across anything connected to this case, I surely would appreciate it if you called me." After giving the information, he left the two women standing in the entrance hall of the Courthouse Museum.

"Such a shame. Just the same as it had been with the other women. Not finding any evidence so they give up. It's always the same with the authorities here," Dorothea added with a sad smile.

"Why don't we ask Crazy Anne? She might know something about it." Her elder friend turned around thinking it was a sarcastic remark from Cheryl but when she saw the young woman's face it didn't show sarcasm but rather worry.

"So, you believe me?"

Cheryl nodded. Only then Dorothea realized how pale her trainee was under her makeup that morning.

"What happened to make you change your mind?"

"I don't see them. But I hear something all the time and yesterday when I walked by that old theater ..."

Her elder friend looked at her, shocked. "The Bird Cage? It calls you, doesn't it?" Cheryl simply nodded.

"Listen, darling, we have to take care of today's business now, but we'll talk tonight. I'll come to your place, if that's okay. You can tell me exactly what happened last night. Don't forget, it was Crazy Anne's home and she might have a thing to say about all this. There is nothing you have to be scared of, except maybe nighttime. This town lives a different life once the sun sets."

The day seemed to drag endlessly, and Cheryl was glad when she could finally lock up at the museum.

She had enough time to shower and prepare a light meal

at her antique home. Dorothea arrived right on time at 7:30, but Cheryl barely recognized her at first.

The lady wore an 1880s-style dress with a bustle, made from beautifully embroidered plaid material. A gorgeous hat in matching colors covered most of Dorothea's hair. She carried a big paper bag.

"What in the world?" Cheryl wondered but her visitor hushed her with an index finger on her lips.

"I brought this bustle dress for you; it should fit. Please try it on."

Cheryl laughed. "Are we going to a costume contest or a saloon or what?"

Her friend was not surprised by the other woman's reaction. "Cheryl, in order to understand the old days and the people who lived here, you should feel like one of them. Communication with the past comes so much easier then. Wearing these clothes might help."

"You've got to be kidding me!"

"Give it a try. You have nothing to lose." Dorothea pulled a beautiful, shiny dress in a rich green color out of the brown paper bag. Cheryl didn't want to offend her friend again and agreed. She took the dress into the bedroom to change. Surprisingly, the skirt and the lace embroidered jacket fit perfectly.

When Cheryl turned and looked at the old-fashioned dressing mirror that resembled the one in the downstairs room at the Bird Cage Theatre, she gasped in disbelief. The reflection in the mirror didn't look like her. She stared into the face of a stranger. A step toward the door caused the silky material to produce a rustling sound. The clothes felt surprisingly comfortable, and the sound of the material seemed familiar.

She walked into the living room where Dorothea waited,

sitting on the antique sofa with a thoughtful expression on her face. "Oh my God, look at you! How beautiful, Cheryl! This outfit is made for you, the color, the fit, simply everything. Good heavens, you look as if you stepped out of the 1880s into this living room."

It felt weird for Cheryl to sit and eat in another woman's clothes but to her surprise she started to feel different wearing them. Even her language changed— Cheryl avoided modern words without being aware of it. For the first time in many months she could not remember where she had left her cell phone. It simply didn't matter.

When the plates were cleared and a pot of fresh coffee set on the table, Dorothea suggested lighting the two antique oil lamps.

"Isn't it dangerous to use them in an old house?" Cheryl wondered.

"No, they work well. I used them quite often and, to be frank, Crazy Anne cannot stand modern electricity."

Cheryl didn't dare question that remark and followed Dorothea's advice. The living room grew darker but the light of the flickering flame spread a warm glow. After a few moments both flames stabilized and they adjusted them slightly.

"Whatever happens now, try to remain open-minded."

Dorothea looked around the room and remained silent for a few moments. When she finally spoke, it made Cheryl jump.

"Crazy Anne, I am sure you have seen my friend Cheryl around in this beautiful house of yours. She loves your home, Anne. My friend here helps me at the museum and is in town to learn the history. You can tell us so much about the old days in Tombstone. Cheryl is bothered by things she hears when she walks around town at night. She sees things in her dreams. Can you explain to us why all this is happening to her?"

The room remained silent. Cheryl didn't know what to expect. When the silence stretched out for several minutes she was about to get up and ask herself what she was doing here dressed as if she had stepped out of a Hollywood studio prop room. Was she actually trying to talk to the ghost of a woman who died in the early 1900s? This was simply ridiculous.

Just when she was about to get up from her chair and call the whole thing off, she heard a soft female whisper. Or did Cheryl's ears fool her again? There! There it was again. Loud and clear.

"The Bird Cage!"

Dorothea looked at Cheryl who stared back at her, her face a mask of disbelief.

She asked into the gloomy living room. "The Bird Cage? What's wrong with it?"

"He is calling her to come back to him," the voice whispered.

"Who wants her back? Is Cheryl called to come to the theater? Why?"

No answer. Cheryl shook her head. Just as both women thought the conversation was over, the whispering voice came again.

"Russian Bill—he wants Mae to come back. He still loves her and needs her. He has been waiting for her all these years. But beware, Hutchinson will not let her go. The greedy pimp Hutchinson needs women for the brothel. He did not want to let her leave in the old days, and he will not let her go now."

"But, Crazy Anne, what does Cheryl have to do with all this?" Dorothea asked into the dark corner from where the voice seemed to come. But there was no answer anymore. Whoever had been whispering to them was gone like a gentle breeze at dawn.

Dorothea stared at Cheryl who had gone pale. What in the world was happening here? Who had been talking to them? The older woman got up and turned on the lights.

Cheryl closed her eyes. The sudden glare of the ceiling fixture blinded her a moment, and she missed the calm, yellowish light of the oil lamps.

The rustle of Dorothea's dress was a comforting sound, but Cheryl's heart pounded in her chest and she couldn't help but rub her arms to chase away the goosebumps.

"What does all this mean? Was she talking about Mae Davenport?"

Her friend sat silently for a moment, sipping on her coffee that had grown cold in its delicate porcelain cup. Cheryl offered to brew a fresh one but Dorothea shook her head at the offer.

"It looks like you have some sort of connection to that historical building or its spirits. It almost sounded as if you have something to do with Mae Davenport." Dorothea mused but the younger woman shook her head.

"I heard the name for the first time a couple of days ago when I read it on a city license at the museum and in a book about the red-light district here."

"However, there has to be some sort of link."

"Who is that Hutchinson guy the voice spoke about?" Cheryl wondered. The name somehow worried her.

"He was the owner of the place. Hutchinson and his wife originally planned to provide theater entertainment for the whole family, but no respectable woman of Tombstone ever set foot in his premises. So, the soiled doves took over the place as their favorite playground, and Hutchinson understood pretty fast that if he allowed those kinds of women to roam the Bird Cage, the men would visit in higher numbers and would spend a lot of money. Most likely, much more than the respectable town couples would.

And that, of course, played right into his pockets. Therefore, he and his wife turned the place into a brothel, saloon, and gambling hall less than four weeks after opening.

"It's said that he got greedy and started to abuse the ladies of the night and would rarely let the very successful ones leave the place again. The sad thing is that many of them died of disease or alcohol abuse or committed suicide. Some of those calico queens also got lucky and found a reasonable man to marry. Hutchinson most likely didn't fancy that, as it meant losing a good pony in his stable, so to speak. I can imagine he must have acted like a dangerous, controlling pimp. After all, there was a lot of money in prostitution."

Cheryl remained silent. Something about this explanation sounded familiar but she couldn't put it into words. The thoughts were stuck as in thick fog and she couldn't quite get hold of them. The feeling vanished as fast as it had appeared.

"Well, it's getting late for an old lady like me." Dorothea stifled a yawn.

Cheryl asked her to wait a moment so she could return the dress but her friend shook her head.

"I don't fit into the dress anymore. You may keep it as a souvenir to remind you of your time here in Tombstone whenever you get ready to leave for California again."

Cheryl touched the skirt gently. "This is an expensive dress. How can I accept such a gift?"

"The color and size fit you much better than it ever fit me. Go on and keep it." Cheryl embraced the elderly woman, deeply touched by her generosity.

She waved goodbye and watched Dorothea drive off toward the courthouse, but she remained standing in front of the house, staring into the darkness, deep in thought, when a male voice made her jump.

"You look so lovely tonight, Mae. I've always loved that color on you." It was the gentle, husky voice she knew well by now. A pleasant tingle moved from her stomach to her chest.

She blushed slightly. The scent of a cherry cigar tingled her nostrils. She saw the shadow of a tall man leaning against the pole of the porch. His hair fell thick and wavy onto his broad shoulders, yet it wasn't moved by the gentle evening breeze. His eyes were hidden in the shadows.

Cheryl should have been scared to death. But to her astonishment she was not, despite the fact that she could see the Courthouse Museum's brick wall down the road shimmering through the handsome figure standing beside her. His face was rather blurry, but nevertheless, she knew it was him and would have recognized him anywhere as the man she had seen during her vision in front of the poker booth.

The silky skirt softly rustled against her legs as she moved toward him. He held his arms wide open for her, and as he pulled her next to his muscular chest, she could finally feel his solid flesh.

The house, the street, and parked cars vanished and the scenery changed. The woman in the green dress found herself on the dusty street in the middle of Tombstone's silver boom years.

CHAPTER 16

* * *

EMBRACING EACH OTHER IN FRONT OF CRAZY ANNE'S HOUSE, THE TWO LOVERS did not hide how deeply they felt for each other.

Crazy Anne waved. She was happy for Mae Davenport. Russian Bill was a good man to have, and it seemed that he finally found his future in the loving arms of Mae. None of the three paid attention to Hutchinson, the owner of the Bird Cage who stood across the road.

His face bore a hateful mask of anger. Hutchinson had changed lately. He had made a fortune by allowing the fallen angels to ply their trade at his premises, and by now the theater attracted famous performers from all over the country. The success had turned him into a greedy individual.

The brothel had a never-ending demand for fresh women. After all, it was the sporting girls that guaranteed the miners would spend their hard-earned silver at the gambling tables and in the sparsely furnished cribs above the stage or down in the basement rooms. The owner was not a fool. He knew that any serious romance developing between a guest and one of his soiled doves would eventually lead to her loss. His intention was to end the love affair between Russian Bill and Mae Davenport. She had become a real magnet to the crowd, especially now that Lizette had developed into an unpredictable drunk with suicidal tendencies. Lizette's laudanum and alcohol abuse had started to show and her beauty was fading, in his opinion. One never knew what that crazy ginger head would do next.

No, Hutchinson was not willing to lose Mae to her Prince Charming. And neither did he want to give up on that Tattenbaum fellow as a regular guest since that European fool spent a fortune renting his poker booth. Who the hell knows? Mae might even talk him into giving up his gambling habit.

The owner of the notorious honky-tonk stomped across the dusty street toward one of the town's shabbier saloons while a devious strategy developed in his evil mind. By the time he entered the tent saloon with its stale odor of old beer and cigar smoke, he had laid out the perfect plan of how to end the liaison between the two love birds.

He would have to sacrifice some income for a short while, but if it worked out the way he planned, he would be the winner in the end. He might be able to keep both of them linked to his theater. All he had to do was make them stop loving each other.

The table at the rear end of the tent was occupied with some mean-looking, unshaved owl hoots who concentrated on their poker game while sharing a bottle of the cheapest, watered-down whiskey available in town.

When Hutchinson reached them, they didn't bother looking up. He pulled a chair to the table and waved at the bartender as he pointed to a bottle of the higher-quality whiskey.

"A hard-working gentleman deserves a better drink and

the company of some beautiful women, don't you think?" Just as expected, he got their attention right away. All three dropped their cards face-down and stared, waiting for him to spill the beans and tell them what he wanted. He was aware that these were true scalawags with nothing much to lose. The procurer, on the other hand, had a lot to lose, so he played it very carefully with them.

"Gentleman, I can offer you an unforgettable week with the most beautiful women of the trade and some money to enjoy some fine whiskey and cigars if you help me get rid of a minor problem."

One of the road agents looked around and pointed at his companions. "This is Jeff, my brother Pete, and I'm Four Fingers Jack, for obvious reason,"

Holding up his left hand, Hutchinson saw that the man's ring finger was missing. As he stared at the man's hand, Four Finger Jack explained, "I held a wrong card in my left hand, and got my finger shot off over it."

"Now why would a card be wrong, and why would someone shoot your finger off?"

"Happened to be the Queen of Hearts, and unfortunately, that card was lying on the table already. Tried to push my luck a bit with a second deck of cards in my vest pocket. But as you see, I managed to escape, thanks to my brother Pete."

The bartender set a bottle of the better corn juice on the table and the three men helped themselves to a generous shot, throwing the lousier quality in their glasses against the canvas wall of the tent. Hutchinson refused the offered glass as he needed to keep his mind clear.

"Okay, Bird Cage pimp, what is it you need from us?"

The sophisticated man squirmed at the name he was called, and looked back at the bartender who was busy on the other side of the tent. After he made sure the guy was not paying attention to their conversation, he spoke barely above a whisper.

"I have this friend of mine who wants to be an outlaw, but I fear for his safety. It would be a good lesson if he could ride with you guys maybe for a small excursion of cattle rustling somewhere in New Mexico. That way he may truly understand what it's like to dodge the law."

Four Finger Jack stared at him and calmly asked, "Are you suggesting that we do something against the law to teach your friend the good and bad sides of outlawing? You've got to be kidding. Why in the world should we get ourselves into a hot spot for the sake of educating a man we don't know?"

Hutchinson had expected that question. "Let's put it this way, the fellow is mighty rich and I'm sure he would share some of his silver coins with you guys if he could ride your brand for a try."

Now he'd gotten their full attention. Most people in this town forgot about their own safety when the call of silver tempted their grabby hearts. So, they decided to take Russian Bill along on a short raid for horses down at the border near Shakespeare, New Mexico.

When the owner of the Bird Cage met Russian Bill at his usual poker spot, he introduced the three saddle tramps, who lured him into the set-up adventure of horse rustling for a few days' ride east of Tombstone.

William Tattenbaum admired the rebellious outlaws but so far Curly Bill and his friends had never taken him seriously enough to let him join their gang. Here was his chance to become a real frontier longrider. He would finally be recognized and admired as a dangerous man. It was his dream to regain some of the respect he had had as an elite soldier of the Russian czar.

He waited until Mae showed up for work and immediately told her that he was supposed to ride on an important mission to Shakespeare. But his lover smelled something fishy about the whole story and didn't like at all that he was so thrilled about it.

Every attempt to stop him from riding with the strangers failed. After spending a passionate night together in his quarters, both parted in the early dawn hours as the gray daylight slowly crawled over the hills full of silver in Tombstone, Arizona.

Mae still felt his touch and lips on her skin when she arrived at the home she shared with the other two girls. She also felt something else—fear.

An hour later the man who owned the most famous house of ill repute in town watched the four riders leave east bound. A satisfied, devilish grin showed on his face while he dropped the lace curtains back into place and turned away from the window of his front parlor.

CHAPTER 17

***

MAE WAS SAD AND RESTLESS THAT EVENING. HER PERFORMANCE ON STAGE was well appreciated as usual, but she didn't entertain any men in the downstairs chamber. She couldn't pin it down, but something seemed suspicious about that sudden offer to her man to join those lowlifes. The gut feeling worried her throughout the whole night. If only she knew what was wrong.

The next day she saw Curly Bill. He smiled at her, and asked her right away why his friend had not appeared at the poker table.

"So, did you wear out poor Bill so that he was unable to show up for our poker game for the first time in months?"

Mae was pale and shook her head. She didn't much like Curly Bill. He was a dangerous man and had carried on more than one hot-tempered discussion with the Earp brothers, who represented the law in Tombstone.

One was well advised not to get on his bad side, people said. But she pulled herself together and told him about the weird incident of the mob of outlaws asking her lover out of the blue to join them.

Curly Bill squinted his eyes and listened in silence. Not that he took his Russian poker partner seriously as a bandito, but he liked the fellow. He was educated, good to talk to, and it was fun to play cards with him. Besides, he always had money to spend. Curly Bill actually trusted the fellow, and that was a rare thing.

Russian Bill's friend agreed something was wrong here, and he didn't like it either. Just like Mae, he felt the story didn't fit together, and decided to ride out of town to find out what this was all about. After all, he hadn't heard of the gang of cowboys planning any horse rustling, and he would have known as their leader, wouldn't he? The whole story sounded like a skin game.

Mae was quite relieved, and thanked him when he promised he'd ride after Russian Bill.

The next two days came and went and she was not her usual cheerful self. Hutchinson pulled her aside and made it clear that he wanted his guests to be entertained in the best possible way. When she told him she wasn't feeling up to it, he became unexpectedly rude.

"Listen to me, you little dancing filly. You were hired to entertain the men in every way, whether you feel up to it or not. In case you're worried about your Russian lover, let me tell you, he probably forgot all about you already and has gone to the next boom town and to the next soiled dove. I overheard him saying he was getting bored with you. Did you really think he was serious about you? You sell your favors for silver. Show me one man who would have respectful thoughts about a woman with such morals. There is not a single prospector who would have serious intentions about spending the rest of his life with you. Russian Bill can have any woman in this house or on Sixth Street. And believe me, he's had many of them already," Hutchinson added with cruel laughter.

His words hurt as if he had slapped her in the face. Was this true? Did he know something she didn't? After all, that pimp had known her beloved Bill longer than she had.

Mae turned and walked through the front door. She was furious and heartbroken. What if he was right? It was possible, wasn't it?

Now that she thought about it, Bill had not stopped to listen to her worries. What in the world had she expected? She should have known better. Blinded by tears, she took a few steps and bumped right into Curly Bill's chest.

"Whoa, hold your horses, little dancing queen, where are you going?"

"Curly Bill! Am I happy to see you."

He laughed. "Dang! It must be over a decade since I've heard a beautiful woman say that."

But his face changed to a serious expression. He took her arm and pulled her to the other side of the road so the guests who were drinking at the long bar couldn't overhear their conversation. Some of them stared at the two of them as they left, but everyone pretended not to pay much attention. No one in town dared to interfere in Curly Bill's business.

"What happened? What's wrong? Where is my man?" Mae could barely hold back her fear. She knew something was wrong and saw it in his eyes.

Curly Bill Brocius looked into her eyes, then cleared his throat. He tried hard to find the right words, and for the first time in many years, didn't want to appear heartless.

"The cowboys Russian Bill rode with were foolish enough to steal some horses from a cattle baron who has quite a few ranch hands. They immediately set up a posse. Four Finger Jack shot one of them and the posse followed them all the way back to the border of the Arizona territory. They caught Pete, Jeff, and Russian Bill. Four Finger Jack escaped."

Mae covered her face with her hands. "So, he's in prison now? When is the trial?"

Brocius shook his head. "The ranch hand that got shot was the rancher's son. They gathered a mob, whipped them into a fury and …"

Mae stared at him not wanting to hear the rest.

"Believe me, Mae, I tried my best but there was no stopping them. It was a hell of a nasty crowd. A sheriff was among the posse, but the mob threatened him with a shotgun. By God, I swear they would have put the lawdog six feet under if he had tried to protect them prisoners. Pete was cursing Hutchinson like crazy."

"Curly Bill, where is my man?" Mae asked through the tears streaming down her cheeks.

"I am sorry, my dear, but I have to tell you that he's dead. They hung him along with the other two fellows. I wished I could have helped him, but it would have been straight suicide, and nobody would have ever changed the mob's opinion about him or the others. The man didn't have the slightest chance. But at least he did not suffer. The rope snapped his neck like a dead branch off a tree when he fell. Bill was dead immediately."

Mae stared at him. She tried to grasp the words but couldn't accept their meaning. She was sure William Tattenbaum—known to all of them as Russian Bill—would ride around the corner onto Allen Street at any moment.

She thought this must be some sort of bad joke. As she glared at Curly Bill Brocius, finally the words pierced her consciousness like painful daggers and they broke her heart.

He was gone. The man she loved deeply and had wanted to spend the rest of her life with would never come back to her. But suddenly she recalled some of Curly Bill's earlier words.

"What did you mean when you said Pete cursed Hutchinson? Why? What has that pimp got to do with all of this?"

The famous gunman looked toward the Bird Cage, his face changing into a dangerously controlled mask, his eyes glittering with hatred.

"He apparently had set them up to lure Russian Bill out of town for a few days."

"What? Why in the world would he do that? He earns a lot of money from Bill who pays him at least twenty silver dollars every night for that one booth next to the stage." She stared at him, not understanding at all what he was trying to tell her.

"You don't get it, do you? That rat loses much more money if his poker-playing client seduces one of his painted ladies to fly into the marriage nest and give up performing her trade in that hell hole over there. That would be a true loss for him. You're one of his best ponies. Just recall the amount your lover paid for you."

Mae blushed. "He told you?" She was deeply embarrassed. The outlaw simply nodded.

"No reason to be ashamed. To find true love is priceless, my dancing fawn."

The devastated calico queen stared into the outlaw's face and finally understood what he was saying. Her lips trembled.

"It was because of me, wasn't it? Hutchinson pulled that nasty trick because of me. My love for Bill has literally killed him. Is that what you're trying to tell me?"

Her pitch had risen, and she became hysterical. Normally that was something Curly Bill couldn't stand from women, but this time he didn't walk away. He embraced her, and at that moment understood how close his friend and the dancing carnival girl Mae Davenport had been.

Yes, they had truly loved each other. And for a brief moment the man holding the sobbing woman envied his dead friend. Of course, he would never let anybody know that. After all, he was Curly Bill Brocius, one of the leaders of the cowboy gangs in Cochise County and feared by many.

"Mae, I need to tell you something else." She slowly turned her gaze upwards, her expression a mask of pure pain.

"When Russian Bill spotted me in the crowd, he begged me to come closer and I did. He told me to let you know that he'll come back to you."

She shook her head. "He's dead, for God's sake! Why would he say such a thing with a rope around his neck?"

"I don't know Mae; I really don't know." He tried to calm her and felt awful that he hadn't been able to save his friend's life. How ironic it was that he had died a real outlaw's death although no one had ever seen him as an outlaw.

She jerked away from him and walked briskly across the street toward the theater's entrance. Standing in the doorway, she screamed Hutchinson's name over and over. Curly Bill wondered what she was up to and took a step across the street to follow, when he realized his big knife was gone from his belt.

"Dang! The crazy woman must have snatched my Bowie." He crossed the street as fast as he could but had to jump back as a stagecoach rolled by, moving quickly. When the path to the Bird Cage cleared, he ran over, afraid she would try to hurt the villain with his knife. Not that Curly Bill cared much for Hutchinson but after all, it was his blade she was planning to use. He'd had enough trouble lately with the lawdogs and didn't need more of it.

"You took everything away from me, Hutchinson! You greedy bastard! He was a good friend to you, paid you a fortune, and you? This is how you thank your pal and regular guest? You set him up with the outlaws to lure my man into a deadly trap!" Mae was madder than a hornet, and she shook her left fist at him.

The owner of the establishment obviously felt uneasy. His small, rat-like eyes darted from one corner to the other. This whole thing had gotten out of hand. He had never wanted his best-paying guest to get lynched by a mob. After all, that love-crazy fool had paid him a fortune for his poker table every night.

What a loss! And here it left him with a hysterical prostitute screaming and waving a hell of a knife in her right hand, and his guests already wondering what the ruckus was all about. If the truth of his dirty dealings against that gambler became known among his guests and in town, he would surely lose a lot of money. It was dangerous for his reputation and business. Not only that, some of Russian Bill's friends might try to take revenge for his death.

He tried to calm the furious woman, raising his hands. "Mae, believe me, I have nothing to do with all of this."

"You're a liar; you're nothing but a varmint who abuses women. There was a witness, right there when they hung my Bill. I curse you, William Hutchinson, I curse you! You are responsible for the death of Russian Bill. I lost everything and may be going to hell but I will take you with me. You shall be damned to stay in this god-forsaken brothel of yours for eternity! You shall never be free, you hear me? Never! May the devil keep you prisoner in this cursed building of yours and never let your soul find peace!"

Mae raised the big knife high above her head, the lights reflected off its sharp blade. Clutching Hutchinson's collar with a final scream that had the onlookers' hairs standing up, she brought down the Bowie knife with one fast slash. Curly Bill tried to stop her, but he didn't reach the rage-blinded woman in time to succeed.

The sickening sound of metal ripping through fabric and flesh seemed unusually loud. The nearby men stood in disbelief, paralyzed for a few seconds. All they saw was Hutchinson lying on the ground and tiny Mae beneath his bloated body.

After a few moments, the crowd reacted and pushed the overweight man off of the slender dancer's body. Everybody expected him to be seriously wounded, but the people at the scene saw that Mae lay on the hardwood floor with the knife stuck in her abdomen, her right hand still holding its wooden grip.

A dark stain had spread on her lovely dress, and she blinked her tears away. The iron-like smell of fresh blood battled against the cigar smoke of the men standing next to the dying woman. Mae raised a bloody hand and touched Hutchinson's face. Her soft whisper was only meant to be heard by him and Curly Bill, who had knelt down beside her.

"I condemn you, William Hutchinson. May your greed hold you prisoner in this theater of yours forever." She smeared her blood onto the man's face. He scrambled back frantically in horror. A shocked hush fell over the crowd. Some crossed themselves.

The man was cursed by a woman who had committed the deadly sin of suicide, not willing to live without the love of her life. Mae's eyes locked with those of Curly Bill.

"He will come back, right? He promised," she whispered.

The gunfighter kneeled next to her and slowly nodded his head, his heart full of sorrow for the dying beauty. He pondered how deeply she must have loved his friend.

She managed a small, shy smile. Then her eyes went blank, staring at the ceiling, no longer seeing the countless bullet holes. Her pretty head rolled gently to the side. The hardwood floor soaked up her blood, leaving a dark stain.

Mae Davenport would never dance at the Bird Cage again. She had left the theater for good but her curse would remain right there within the famous walls.

CHAPTER 18

***

CHERYL OPENED HER EYES AS SHE SAT IN THE ROCKING CHAIR ON THE FRONT
porch. She couldn't remember having fallen asleep or how
long she had been out. It was dark and she felt cold.

She still wore the green dress Dorothea had given to her
and felt depressed, a pang of great loss. Cheryl rose and
walked into the house. This time she remembered every
detail of her dream, and a sadness like she had never known
almost choked her.

When Cheryl arrived at work the following day, Dorothea was shocked at how pale and tired she looked. Dark
circles showed under her eyes.

"Girl, what's the matter with you? Did yesterday's
events scare the wits out of you? You look as if you've
seen a ghost or something."

The younger woman shrugged her shoulders. "Well, I
guess that's exactly what happened. I saw Russian Bill, or
more accurately, he paid me a visit. He's the one whose
voice and cherry cigar smoke follows me all around town.
Frankly, I'm quite sure I'm losing my mind."

Dorothea poured her friend a fresh cup of coffee. It

was a weekday and the museum hadn't been busy the past few days.

"What exactly has happened, and what do you mean, you saw him?"

Cheryl sat down, stifled a yawn, and told Dorothea everything, including her dream. When she finished, her heart was pounding so hard in her chest that she was pretty sure that her motherly friend could hear it.

The elder lady remained silent for a moment and was obviously surprised at how fast events had developed since their evening together. The story of Mae Davenport committing suicide before the front bar of the Bird Cage was extremely unnerving.

Dorothea knew that certain men had been killed in the building over a deck of cards or during a heated argument among the miners and buckaroos. It was not astonishing that people thought that the building was haunted.

But this death had a different outcome with Mister Hutchinson being damned. Was Mae's curse the reason why his restless soul still tried to call women back to work for him as ladies of the night? Could it be that the theater continued to exist as a notorious honky-tonk despite being turned into a museum decades ago?

Whatever had happened there, one thing was sure— the events of the past few weeks had changed Cheryl, and Dorothea was starting to worry tremendously for her friend's safety. This was going beyond anything she or her husband had experienced in Tombstone so far.

That evening back in her guest house, the California student ate a sandwich, although she didn't feel hungry at all. She couldn't say what was wrong with her, but since that terrible dream the night before she felt an extreme sadness and a longing for the man whose shadowy figure she had seen standing on her porch.

Cheryl didn't question what was happening in this weird little Western town any longer. All she knew was that she belonged here and that her life in California would never be the same if she returned there.

She showered, dressed in her favorite sweatshirt, and curled up on the couch. As she zapped through all of the TV channels, her thoughts returned to the unhappy ending of the frontier love story. She turned the set off.

All of the movies and shows seemed too loud, too annoying, so she lit the petroleum lamp and turned off the lights in the kitchen and living room.

Now, that's better. She picked up the second book that she bought a few days ago. But nothing distracted her long enough to stop her thoughts from traveling back to the masculine figure and handsome face of Russian Bill's spirit, and she caught herself trying to recall the sound of his voice whispering to her.

Oh my God, I wonder what making love to him would be like. I don't believe in ghosts, and here I go fantasizing about a spirit of an 1880s gambler. How ridiculous is that, Girl!

"Mae, why do you doubt what you see with your own eyes? Why don't you accept what you hear with your own ears?"

Where in the world had that voice come from, here in the house?

"Darling, do you really think that walls could be a boundary for me when I can easily pass the distance of a hundred and thirty-six years?"

Cheryl closed her eyes for an instant. "Bill, is that you?" she asked with a timid voice.

The answer came immediately as a cool breeze gently touched her right cheek. It felt like the caress of a feather.

Soon she saw his shadow sitting next to her. She wanted to reach out with her hand but he motioned her to stop.

"Mae, I am in the dark world of the shadows. You are here in the future Tombstone with your flesh and blood—so warm, so alive. We cannot be together until you cross from your world to the other side."

"What do you mean? Explain it to me, please." But he was vanishing already. She tried to hold him back and sobbed, "Please, Bill! Come back. Explain it to me."

But he was gone, and Cheryl was left behind, lonely and confused in the small house that had belonged to Crazy Anne.

The next few days passed without anything unusual happening, and she was caught in the familiar routine of museum work and meeting people in Tombstone.

By now Cheryl was considered a member of the local population, although everybody knew she planned to return to California in late October.

Cheryl looked at Tombstone very differently now compared to the first few days of her stay. Okay, she admitted that there were some real weirdos living in town and it seemed like some folks were stuck in their life of reenactment. Countless people in this Western settlement seemed to have given up their true identity, and some actually seemed as if they had never had an identity of their own. Cheryl was also aware of the many alcoholics and crystal meth addicts and felt sorry for them.

Without realizing it, an acceptance for the dark side of Tombstone had found its place in Cheryl's heart.

On her day off she strolled up and down Allen Street, but tried her best to avoid the eerie historical brothel. Why, she didn't know for sure but it had to do with the growling voice that had called her back to work the other day and which still made her shiver with fear when she thought of it.

She passed a shop next to the creepy building. She had never noticed it before. As she walked by the entrance door someone called her name.

"Cheryl, would you wait a second?"

She stopped in her tracks, surprised that the lady walking toward her from the back of the store knew her name. But this was Tombstone, a small-town community.

"Hi there, sorry to holler at you like that. I'm Nora." The lady with the dark, gray-streaked hair shook her hand.

"Cheryl. Pleasure to meet you. What can I do for you?"

"Would you join me in the store for a minute? I'll explain," Nora said pointing inside.

She followed the storekeeper, but felt a little uncomfortable. When they reached a small lounge area in the back of the shop, the lady offered her a cup of coffee.

The store displayed refreshments and souvenirs in the front part of the building but the back area was filled with sage, pendulums, tarot cards, and a tee-shirt rack.

What a weird mixture, Cheryl thought. She saw a door going off to the left and wondered what was behind it. *Most likely a staff toilet,* she mused.

"Wrong. It's the entrance to the part of the structure known as the old morgue," Nora said as she handed Cheryl a Styrofoam cup of steaming coffee. "Help yourself with sugar and creamer if you need any."

Cheryl stared at the woman. *How in the world did Nora know that she thought it was the toilet?* Nora pointed to the door.

"Most people come here to do paranormal investigations. The place is pretty active even during the daytime. The shop is only a side business."

Oh, crap. Cheryl thought. That was all she needed right

now. *Here you go, a shopping trip at the haunted morgue.* But she didn't want to be rude. So, she sipped her coffee and waited for Nora's explanation as to why she had called her into the place.

"As I said, in the old days, this was a full-time morgue. Enough killings happened daily in Tombstone and that kept the undertakers real busy.

They had at least two or three full-time morticians working here. Imagine, busy San Francisco at that time had only one undertaker. There was another building between the Bird Cage and us, but that's long gone. Our building is a paranormal hot spot so to speak, so we offer ghost tours daily."

The owner of the place saw Cheryl's face full of doubts, and pointed to the door. "Come with me and you'll understand." She set down her own coffee cup and walked toward the cream-colored, wooden door. It opened to a small rustic bar area and a bigger room which looked like a compact indoor theater.

Cheryl walked along the hardwood floor that creaked under her shoes and studied the pictures on the walls. She saw a big red curtain that was used to block out the daylight. The atmosphere was chilly, and the student felt as if she were being watched. But that was, of course, nonsense, she told herself. Nora looked at her.

"Last night we did a late-night session, and during that paranormal investigation your name was mentioned by a spirit called Crazy Anne. She used to be one of the Bird Cage girls but from the look on your face I assume you already know very well who Crazy Anne is, don't you?"

Cheryl swallowed but could not speak. She nodded her head.

"Take a seat, please."

Since Cheryl was off from work with no appointments to rush to, she sat down on one of the chairs around a simple wood table. The room was gloomy. *Bright daylight most likely would not have been appropriate in an old morgue*, Cheryl assumed. Nora regarded her with her huge gray eyes, and her face showed a serious expression.

"I reckon you don't know much about paranormal activities, right?"

"Jesus, I don't even know if I should believe the things I see with my own eyes lately, to be frank," Cheryl exclaimed. She let her hands fall back into her lap in a helpless gesture.

"I see. Well, let me explain," the friendly lady said. "Most people think in the past, present, or future contexts, which is generally correct. But what they don't know is that past and present are in existence on a parallel level."

"How is that possible?" Cheryl asked.

Nora placed two strips of photo negatives on the table.

"We think way too one-dimensionally. But the world and life are multidimensional, in the sense that the past doesn't necessarily have to end because the present has started. As a matter of fact, the past still exists. At least, for the spirits it does. They contact us here in the present day, but many of them actually still live in their old times and in their old lives."

"That's crazy. Simply not possible."

Cheryl felt as if Nora was joking, yet she knew that the woman was describing an astonishing fact that she had been witnessing lately herself.

As the shop owner continued, she had Cheryl's full attention. "There are places in this world that are hot spots for paranormal activity. We call them 'Crossovers' or 'Gateways.' It could be a battlefield, an area where a disaster had occurred, or a building, for instance. People often think that the cemeteries are the most haunted places. But they're actually not.

"Instead, it's the places where people have lived or died to which their restless souls may return. See these two negatives?" She pointed to the strips on the table. "A paranormal gateway is similar to the two negatives. When I put one on top of the other, both pictures shine through, not completely and not clearly, but visible to both sides.

"This is what happens at such hot spots, and it's exactly what happens at the Bird Cage Theatre, as well as here at the morgue. It's as if the mirror of the present time becomes a transparent veil which gives us a small glimpse into the past, and a few gifted people can actually look through that veil. But it's a crossover that works both ways to a certain extent. That is the reason why some among us are able to see or hear the ones on the other side. Crazy Anne told me last night that Russian Bill calls you because you may be Cheryl in this modern time, but your body seems to hold the soul of the woman formerly known as Mae Davenport."

Cheryl shook her head. Her common sense wouldn't allow her to believe the obvious. "You know what I think? I think everybody in this town has gone crazy believing all this stuff."

Cheryl was about to rush out of the room when the weird lady called her back. Her voice was calm and barely above a whisper.

"He wanted so much to stay and to feel your touch last night but couldn't. He is still caught on the other side of the mirror, and only a living person can cross to the other side for good. Russian Bill is a prisoner in the world of shadows. But he said he felt your hand reaching out to him yesterday."

"How do you know about last night?" Cheryl whispered. *This isn't possible, or is it?*

The store keeper said, "I hope you know what that means. There's no way Russian Bill can be with you as long as you are alive. But I have no doubt that you are indeed Mae Davenport."

Cheryl stared at the woman who slowly got up and walked back to the door to the main store. She followed her, cup in her hand but long forgotten. The younger visitor was confused but thanked Nora and promised to come back for one of the evening tours soon.

Cheryl walked to her accommodation and didn't pay attention to any of the people walking or driving by. Nora's words suddenly hit home: "He can never be with you as long as you are alive. Only the living can cross to the other side for good."

How could it be that Cheryl felt as if she had lost her lover a second time and couldn't do anything to fix it? *How is it possible that I miss him with such a yearning and a physical hunger unlike anything I have ever experienced before? How had it been for Mae to feel his body? How would it be for me to make love to him?*

If only he were alive. Jesus, could she actually believe that she was the reborn Mae Davenport, or that a former lover had returned as a ghost to bring her back home? *Am I losing my mind here in this god-forsaken dusty Western town?*

Cheryl decided to return to the shop called "Paranormal Sisters" for an evening appointment of ghost hunting at the old morgue. She grabbed her phone to call the number on the card Nora had given her as she had to find more answers.

The friendly lady signed her up for the late-hour group after 10:00 p.m. and said how thrilled she was that Cheryl would be joining them.

CHAPTER 19

***

WALKING BACK TO THE OLD MORGUE SHE KNEW THAT SHE HAD TO GET UP EARLY for work the following day but didn't mind. At 9:30 p.m., she stepped through the door and smelled a bad sulfur odor like rotten eggs. That odor hadn't been there in the afternoon, and Cheryl wrinkled her nose, which Nora noticed.

"You smell it too, don't you?"

"Yeah, what in the world is it?"

Nora looked toward the other room. "Some spirits are pretty evil. They carry a stench like that. The morgue seems to be outstandingly active tonight. The 8:00 o'clock tour was so full of activity that one lady had a panic attack and left. Guess she's over at Doc Holliday's bar now trying to recover from her shock. This stuff can freak some people out."

They both laughed. About ten minutes later, another four tourists walked into the place. They all had booked the same tour and were pretty excited, chatting nervously. When the group was complete, Nora locked the front door and turned on an emergency light. All other lights had to be switched off. Their host welcomed the group and led them into the adjoining room.

Nora explained the history of the morgue, and how rowdy the past had been during the silver boom time. She showed them the room where dead bodies had been embalmed as well as the mortician equipment and explained the undertaker's job in those days.

It was horrifying for some of the tourists. There was a wooden box filled with square bottles containing original embalming fluids.

"We are actually pretty lucky to have found a lot of the original equipment still stored in this building."

At the end of the informational tour, Nora led the group into the main room across a small rustically built bar and asked everyone to sit down around the big table. She handed out different electronic devices that were supposed to catch temperature changes or unusual electrical static. It was the kind of equipment one would see in TV shows about the paranormal.

She placed one flashlight on the table and one on the mortician's table that stood a few feet away from the guests next to the bar. They were switched on, and none of the visitors were close enough to touch them. Nora set up her laptop and started a voice recorder program.

She spoke into the gloomy room. The laptop screen cast a ghostly light on her face.

"Hello, ladies and gentlemen of the building. We want to greet you as respectful visitors. Would you like to communicate with us today?"

Cheryl had her doubts that this exercise would work the way it was expected. She was still extremely skeptical about the whole topic of ghost hunting. But then she recalled the weird evening when she and Dorothea had tried to get in touch with Crazy Anne's spirit who had actually spoken to them.

As Cheryl's thoughts wandered, the flashlight on the table started flickering, and the light died. *The battery is probably done for the day.*

They could see the mortician's table through the connecting doorway into the adjoining room. At first, the guests couldn't believe what they saw. The second flashlight slowly rolled back and forth over the surface of the table.

An excited murmur rose among the group. Nora kept speaking to those spirits she assumed to be present. A crackling sound came from the laptop speakers. At first Cheryl thought it must be static distortion of some kind, but then single words spoken by different voices could be heard. The employee of the Courthouse Museum immediately recognized one very angry voice. It growled in the darkness again and again the words, "She cursed me."

Nora asked the voice. "Who cursed you?"

"It was her! Mae!"

Cheryl whispered into Nora's ear "Hutchinson?" but the elder woman shrugged her shoulders. There were giggles of a woman, the rowdy laughter of another male voice, and then the voice Cheryl would have recognized anywhere.

"Mae, come back to me."

She swallowed hard. That must be the voice of Russian Bill. Immediately she felt her cheeks blush, and her heart skipped a beat or two.

Nora watched her closely.

The other group members started to ask questions but except for single words, some of them barely understandable, no further answers came. After thirty minutes Nora called the session off. The tourists left through the front store, chatting excitedly. They obviously had experienced what they had expected for their money.

Nora motioned Cheryl to stay back while she said good-bye to the other guests and thanked them for participating. She turned around and lit some sage she took from a metal bowl standing behind the counter. It developed some white smoke and smelled pleasant. Nora waved the smoke all over Cheryl and said some sort of prayer.

When she saw the woman's confused face, the host of the paranormal tour told her that sage was used for spiritual cleansing, which was important after communicating with spirits. Cheryl asked Nora why she had not cleansed the others.

"Simply because you were the target of the spirits that showed up today. By the way, I believe that the angry sounding one was indeed Hutchinson but there was another spirit standing behind you, a handsomely shaped figure, as far as I could tell from the shadow. I smelled cherry cigars on him. He was the reason Hutchinson could not attack you any further. You recognized his voice, didn't you?"

Cheryl looked away, a painful expression on her face. "Yes," she whispered. "I think it was Russian Bill."

"I thought as much," Nora said. "Well, time to close this place up and go home. In case you have any questions or want to come back again for a chat, with me or with them, you know where to find us all."

Cheryl thanked her and slowly walked out of the building. As she glanced to the right, the Bird Cage hovered over her like a dark spider waiting in its web.

She was bewildered. On one hand, the place pulled her toward its entrance and she sensed happy days inside. On the other, the building scared her since she knew that Mae died by her own hand in the front room.

She turned around, watched Nora lock the door and waved goodnight, and walked slowly along the deserted street toward her Victorian home.

Without realizing it Cheryl waited until she smelled the beloved tobacco flavor she had gotten so used to during the past weeks. She was not at all worried when she saw a second shadow trailing her on the sandy dirt road. He was with her and his presence warmed the lonely woman walking in the chilly night air.

When Cheryl arrived home, she looked over to the shadow and whispered, "I know you can't touch me and sadly I can't feel you either. But maybe you can find a way to be with me in my sleep. It might be possible to be in my dreams, right?" He looked back at her, his face still blurry like a wavering picture, but he smiled and promised that he would try.

She showered and went to bed. Her sleep was rather a tossing-and-turning matter, and again and again she heard Hutchinson's angry voice blaming her for cursing him.

Despite being exhausted she woke a couple of times covered in her own cold sweat. Finally, long after 3:00 a.m. she fell into a deep slumber. And then Russian Bill found his way to enter her dreams and to make her feel his warm embrace and caresses through the barrier of time like it used to be in the old days.

CHAPTER 20

* * *

NORA, WHO OWNED THE OLD MORGUE, CALLED DOROTHEA AND TOLD HER ABOUT the events of the paranormal session the previous night. Now the museum manager and her husband worried even more about Cheryl.

She spoke to Bert about all the things that had happened in the last few days. He was concerned, too. He knew that certain things in Tombstone were not easily explained, but this was far beyond what he and his wife had experienced since moving to town.

"What can we do? Should we encourage Cheryl to return to California?" Bert looked at his better half, waiting for an answer.

"That is Cheryl's decision, and of course that of the Arizona State Parks as well. Unless we inform the board of directors of some wrongdoing, they would never fire Cheryl since she is on a study internship. But Cheryl has done nothing wrong."

Bert knew his wife was right about that. Like most people in town they would hate to see her leave Tombstone ahead of her scheduled departure. *What if the girl is in extreme danger,* he wondered.

The next day at work, Cheryl showed up paler than ever. But there was a smile on her face and her eyes were shining despite being red and bloodshot. Obviously, she had not slept much but did not seem to be tired. She was rather thrilled as if something exciting had happened to her. However, when Dorothea asked about it, she avoided answering.

Bert looked at their employee, a confused expression on his face. Later he asked if Dorothea thought Cheryl wasn't well. "Do you think she takes drugs?" His spouse shook her head but couldn't come up with a decent answer.

At closing time, the manager of the museum called Cheryl over to the side exit to join him as he locked up the courtyard. His face stern, he said, "Cheryl, you know we've taken a liking to you. If there is something that bothers you, I hope you know you can talk with us any time."

She tried to avoid his gaze.

"One thing is sure—you've got a spooky little town here." It should have sounded like a joke.

"Do you remember when I told you that Tombstone speaks to some people in dramatic ways?"

"Yeah, I remember."

He touched her shoulder lightly. Her skin was cold despite the warming evening sun. "Sometimes that can be dangerous. Not every spirit in this town is a good one. This is not some sort of fancy California game, Cheryl. If you underestimate the dark side of Tombstone you may be in more danger than you could ever imagine."

Cheryl stared at him and was about to turn away, trying to shrug him off. But when she looked over his shoulder, she saw a man dangling on the rope on one of the gallows. His eyes were empty sockets, and his rotting, black tongue hung out of his mouth.

She felt nauseous and looked into Bert's face, interpreting his expression as a knowing one. *He must be aware of the horrible sight on the gallows,* She thought. *He must have seen the horrifying image countless times.*

Bert held her, while she wept like a small child, leaning against his shoulder. When they walked back into the courthouse to lock up the place, he suggested to his wife that Cheryl should stay overnight at their house. Dorothea quickly agreed, and the confused student was glad not to be alone. She went to her house and packed an overnight bag. It was urgent for her to get away from Allen Street, away from the Bird Cage, and Crazy Anne's house for a day or two.

The two McEntires were extremely kind and generous people and they did their best to make Cheryl feel comfortable. She ended up staying for three nights. But on the fourth day she told them she would return to her house. It wasn't her style to be a burden to anybody. Since no nightmares and no spirits had bothered her, she wondered if her peaceful sleep had anything to do with the sage Dorothea had burned every evening.

Cheryl entered the quiet house on the fourth evening and decided to go to bed early. She wasn't hungry and turned in right after a shower. Despite being under the covers, she felt cold and shivered. But she was too tired to get back up and turn the heater on. Instead Cheryl pulled the covers all the way up to her chin. However, it seemed the temperature in the room dropped further. As she turned to switch off the nightstand lamp a scream escaped her lips.

A woman in a burgundy bustle dress looked down at her, a sad expression on her face. Cheryl was about to jump out of bed but didn't dare move. Was this Crazy Anne? But no, a few seconds later she recognized the pretty face and the long coppery hair.

"My God, have mercy! You're Lizette, aren't you?" Cheryl whispered. The woman smiled at her.

"Good evening, Mae. It's good to see you back. He's so happy, Russian Bill is."

Cheryl shook her head. "Stop this. I don't want to hear any more of this madness. My name is Cheryl, and all of this is not actually happening. I will return to California soon and have a good life there."

But Lizette simply shook her head.

"He stood by his promise and came back. Russian Bill has waited for your return all these years at the Bird Cage. Every night, Mae! We all have waited for you. When you cursed Hutchinson that fateful night and killed yourself, you chained your own soul to the building, same as us."

Only then did Cheryl see the scars on Lizette's wrists and remembered she had read that "The Flying Nymph" committed suicide.

"The Bird Cage is our home, Mae! Russian Bill is your man. It is your time to return now."

Cheryl stared at the woman but before she could protest, the image faded away, and she doubted that she had really seen Lizette. Suddenly a slight breeze from the bathroom moved one of the tiny black feathers that had been sewn to the sleeves of Lizette's dress. It danced lazily in the air before it landed softly on top of her bed covers.

Cheryl hid under the covers crying, feeling helpless like a child and didn't know how to escape this sheer madness that had obviously taken over her life.

When she woke, she felt as if a truck had run over her. She made some strong coffee and sat on the porch steps. The sun was rising but its warmth failed to calm the chills and smooth the goosebumps on her skin.

What was she going to do? She seriously considered leaving town. This whole ghost scene was too much for her to bear. *I must talk to Dorothea and Bert even if I disappoint them by wanting to leave my assigned job so early.*

Feeling torn and guilty, the devastated woman could not bring herself to admit that it wasn't only the McEntire couple she would feel sorry to leave. *God have mercy. I carry a man in my heart who has been dead over one hundred thirty years. How in the world is that possible?*

Cheryl shook her head and walked back into the house to get ready for work. When she arrived at the Courthouse Museum, one look was enough for Dorothea to understand that things had gotten worse again the previous night. Her friend seemed distracted and pale, and she held her tight for a few moments. During lunch Bert and Dorothea took Cheryl out to the O.K. Café and spoke to her like parents would.

"My dear, we see you're suffering and we worry about you. Bert and I have been thinking about sending you home, back to California." When Cheryl started to protest, Bert hushed her.

"We are very happy with your work, and we truly love you, almost like a daughter. But we are very scared for your safety. Somehow, you seem to trigger much more paranormal action here than anybody else has before you. There is something about you that the spirits seek, and we fear that we don't have enough power to protect you, even with Nora's help. We would never forgive ourselves if anything happened to you."

Dorothea looked at Cheryl, tears in her eyes.

"We'll take care of your flight arrangements and make sure that the Arizona State Parks Board receives a proper explanation about your leaving earlier than scheduled."

Cheryl felt a lump in her throat. She never thought this

would happen and didn't really want to leave Tombstone. She had gotten used to the town, its old buildings, and the weird people and rowdy saloons but also knew that Bert was right about her being in some sort of danger.

So, in tears and with a heavy heart she finally agreed to take a direct flight to L.A. the coming weekend. She needed a few days to arrange an accommodation in California as her apartment was rented out to a fellow student for at least another two months and also a bit of time to finish her essays.

When she returned to Crazy Anne's historic house that night, she swallowed a pill to guarantee deep sleep right away. Cheryl didn't want any more of those fitful dreams or visions of ghosts. All she wanted was to be at peace, as she felt emotionally drained.

The pharmaceutical product did its work, and her sleep was dreamless for nine hours straight without waking. However, she was not alone in the room. Russian Bill sat next to her and stroked her hair. His body left no imprint on the bed sheets. He looked sad.

It was the darkest hour before dawn. The Bird Cage lay in shadows except for the emergency exit lights. Hutchinson's rude voice boomed through the crowded bar area as he mocked Russian Bill.

"Your little filly won't come back to you it seems. So, I am the one who wins after all."

The handsome William Tattenbaum stared at his opponent through gray-blue, steely eyes. Hutchinson's face was a mask of pure hatred. When he turned around his features showed the print of a slender hand on his left cheek.

The marks were the same color of crimson as the big stain spreading on the floor in front of the bar. It was there, reappearing again and again like it had so many nights since 1882.

CHAPTER 21

***

THE DATE OF THE FLIGHT BACK TO CALIFORNIA WAS SET, AND CHERYL HAD ONLY another three days remaining in Tombstone. She decided to visit Nora and to thank her for her help. The shop owner stood behind her counter filling out an order sheet when Cheryl walked into the store.

"Hey girl, what are you up to?" Nora smiled.

Cheryl shrugged her shoulders. "Nothing much. To be honest, I came to say goodbye. I'm leaving town day after tomorrow."

Nora murmured, "You're afraid, aren't you?"

"Yes, or let's say, I need to have a good night's rest without seeing all this crazy stuff."

However, the other lady was no fool. Although Cheryl tried to play things down, it was apparent she was terrified. Nora opened one of the glass displays, bringing out a small pendant with an attractive crystal and gently placed it into Cheryl's hand.

"This will protect you. Wear it as long as you are here or even better, wear it all the time. It's my farewell gift to you."

The surprised woman weighed the light blue crystal in her hand. She pulled the thin leather cord over her head. It seemed warm on her chest despite the fact that it was a cool crystal. She thanked Nora and hugged her hard.

"One day, I will visit you again."

The elder woman's gaze followed her out the door. "I hope and pray you never come back, girl!" she whispered.

Nora worried that it was too late for Cheryl to save herself and didn't like the increased activity in the old morgue during the past few weeks. No, she didn't like it at all, and had told that to a few people including Dorothea.

The following day Cheryl decided to pay one last visit to the haunted theater. Most of her stuff was packed for the next day's flight, and she was off work before going to her farewell dinner with Bert and Dorothea.

Returning to the loud and bustling city of L.A. was not something to look forward to. Cheryl wasn't the same person she was when she first set foot in this Western frontier town many weeks ago. She had seen and experienced things that changed her life.

It was mystifying that she felt so comfortable in the historic Bird Cage, but at the same time knew she would feel out of place in L.A. the next day. What was happening to her?

Cheryl bought a ticket at the entrance to the museum. She didn't know the lady on duty and didn't mind paying. She saw a dark stain on the floor in front of the bar. *Maybe it is only a shadow from the bright daylight seeping through the open door? Maybe I see these things because my imagination is in overdrive?*

Fortunately, the place wasn't busy as she had come at a late hour. Most tourists were either on their way out of town or in one of the restaurants and saloons for an early dinner. Generally, the last two hours of the work day most stores or museums weren't crowded, especially during the week days.

When Cheryl entered the gloomy back room with the big stage and the cribs below the ceiling, she felt like she was coming home. She immediately walked to the poker booth next to the stage. A cherry cigar lay burning in a small glass ashtray.

"Bill!" she called but there was no answer. She walked behind the stage and avoided eye contact with the funeral hearse. It still made her uneasy to look at it. The wooden stairs creaked as she took them down to the basement bordello. The sound seemed unnaturally loud. When the lone visitor reached the first chamber, she felt the gentle touch of a breeze caressing her neck line.

The voice whispered into her ear. "Why are you leaving me, Mae? I kept my promise like I told you I would. Why do you betray my love?"

Cheryl didn't know what to say. Tears pooled in her eyes as she turned her head toward the shadow next to her.

"It's not possible. You are in your world, the dark world, and I am here. I want to be with you but I can't even touch you. If I stay here, I'll lose my mind. There is no other way."

Weeping bitterly, she left the museum through the gift shop. But the ghost of Russian Bill didn't follow .

Cheryl soon sat at the table with Bert and Dorothea. The food was delicious, but she had lost her appetite. To say goodbye to the old brothel and Russian Bill had been devastating and heartbreaking.

The friendly couple tried their best to cheer their guest up and to involve Cheryl in bubbling small talk about

God and the whole world but somehow the woman opposite them couldn't pull herself out of her gloomy mood. Around nine, Cheryl excused herself, fibbing that she still had some packing to do.

She just wanted to be alone. Bert dropped her off at the charming historic house Cheryl had called home during the past three months and gave her one of his bear hugs.

"Sleep well, little L.A. cowgirl," he whispered. "Don't be sad, we will always be your friends, and hey, we might come to see you in Los Angeles next spring."

Cheryl hugged him back and thanked him for the nice evening and the ride. Bert and Dorothea had promised to pick her up around noon the next day for the airport transfer to Tucson.

By the time the sad Cheryl had showered it was late, and she sat in her rocking chair on the porch, wrapped in a warm sweater and wearing old faded denims. Loneliness held her heart in its cold grip. She wasn't aware of the fact that she was waiting for him, sniffing the night air for the familiar smell of cherry cigar smoke like a puppy. But Russian Bill didn't appear or talk to her.

He must feel betrayed, Cheryl thought. In bed, she snuggled under the cozy covers recalling the past crazy weeks in Tombstone. All of the weird things that had happened seemed so unreal.

Oh, how much I miss him. Now she knew why she had waited for her Prince Charming, why it had to be a long-haired fellow with gray eyes. *My subconscious must have remembered Russian Bill's handsome features and long wavy hair all these years.* Maybe her soul was still longing for the love of her life, of a time gone by so long ago.

She closed her eyes, trying to get some sleep while wishing more than anything that she could see him and hear him one last time before leaving tomorrow.

Leaving—never in her life had that word sounded so cruel, so unbearable. She had waited in vain for him and she had lost it all. *I can't recall ever feeling so lonely in my entire life.*

CHAPTER 22

* * *

IT WAS PAST MIDNIGHT. THE BUILDING WAS EMPTY. A SHADOW SAT IN THE POKER booth next to the stage. The day's tourists had left and the spirits of the ladies and gentlemen invisible to most human beings remained silent that night.

They shared one emotion in common, the grief over a lost life, a fortune gone, and the loss of love. They were hell-bound and caught in the building that had become their destiny for eternity.

Russian Bill shuffled the cards, his cigar untouched in the crystal ashtray. Helplessly his soul had to accept the fact that he had no way to reach the woman that once had been the love of his short life. The handsome gambler had failed to hold her back in Tombstone.

Cheryl flipped through the pages of the book named "Soiled Doves of the West." Sleep simply would not come. She looked at the photos of long forgotten times. Women in daring clothes captured in their most private moments, lingered in tempting poses.

The picture of Lizette was haunting. What a beautiful woman she had been, but how tragically her life had ended.

Yet Cheryl envied her a little because she had known Mae and Russian Bill, Crazy Anne, and Curly Bill in person, and even more so, Lizette was still able to be with them. *I, the spoiled California girl, am not that lucky* she thought. No, she had to return to a world that meant nothing to her anymore. Jealousy rushed through her like a burning fire. As she stared at the black and white portrait of Lizette with her gorgeous long red hair, a thought crossed her mind.

My God, the solution to all her problems had been right there, reachable all this time. *There is indeed a way to turn back time. I just didn't see it, being too busy with denying the plain facts. My ability to observe a problem from every angle obviously had been lost for a while.*

She chuckled at herself. Now she knew what she had to do. There was a way out of this misery.

She jumped out of bed and stood in front of the antique dressing mirror wearing only her underwear. Cheryl pinned up her hair with two old fashioned combs she had bought in one of the shops a few days back.

She turned around and opened her suitcase. It was packed to the limit. She'd surely have to pay extra for excess weight but didn't mind. "Didn't have that problem during old stagecoach times I guess," Cheryl laughed to the empty room.

With an almost tender caress she touched the skirt and jacket that Dorothea had given her. The shimmering material rustled softly as she unpacked it from her luggage, the luggage of a different time and a different life.

She stepped into the skirt. It fell billowing around her ankles. She put on her shoes and slipped into the embroidered jacket with its tiny silk-covered buttons. The beautiful woman glanced into the mirror, her face looking thinner and pale.

Cheryl smoothed the lace collar around her neck and put on an antique-looking choker with matching earrings. She was pleased with what she saw in the mirror. *How astonishing. I resemble the reflection I've seen in the mirror of the first chamber at the Bird Cage.*

Cheryl's cell phone lay on the bedside table with her purse. She put the crystal Nora had given her next to her phone. She wouldn't need either one tonight and had no use for modern communication techniques where she was going.

The beautifully clad lady stepped out of the house and left the property through the garden gate. She set one foot in front of the other, listening to each hollow clack caused by her heels, but her pace didn't lack confidence even though it was dark.

Cheryl chose the back road behind Allen Street so she wouldn't run into run into anybody. Her worries were in vain. No one was on the street. It was well past midnight, and as usual on a weekday the town was deserted.

There was a chill in the late night air, but Cheryl didn't feel it. The cold wind went through the fabric of her jacket. but it didn't matter. All she could think of were Russian Bill's blue-gray eyes, and the love shining in them.

Walking confidently, she passed the area that had been Tombstone's famous red-light district in the 1880s. Cheryl looked gorgeous in her dress with her dark hair pinned up, almost like an entirely different woman. A gentle smile lit up her face. A few stubborn curls of her hair had freed themselves from the combs.

Finally, she arrived at the Bird Cage. The building lay in complete darkness. The only light source came from a streetlight on the opposite corner. It was nearly 1:00 a.m. on October 28th.

Cheryl stood in front of the main door and took a deep breath. Over one hundred thirty-six years ago on the very same date a dark-haired woman stormed into the notorious premises through that very door.

A soft breeze ruffled her long skirt. Cheryl turned and took a last glance at the cars parked close by, a last peek at the souvenir shops and saloons. Now Cheryl saw them, the shadows of townsfolk long gone, walking along the boardwalk, but did not fear them any longer.

Cheryl Roberts turned back to the door and gently pushed against it, not at all surprised that it swung open for her. She had been certain that the theater would welcome her back home. As Cheryl stepped through the front door, she left the modern world behind, but it did not bother her at all as she was where she belonged. She was Mae Davenport. Cheryl Roberts was not important anymore. All that counted was Russian Bill and a carnival dancer named Mae.

CHAPTER 23

***

THE ROOM WAS FILLED WITH THE LOUD ROAR OF THE CROWD AND THE PIANO playing a polka from the Old World. The men at the bar toasted her, their glasses filled with whiskey. The booth next to the stage was empty. Nobody shuffled the cards there but Mae didn't worry about it. She knew he was waiting for her in the very same room where they had made love the first time. All she had to do was walk downstairs. With a knowing smile the beautiful woman stepped behind the stage and was on her way to the basement …

***

The next morning the museum employee Heather opened the front door to the Bird Cage Theatre. Somehow the lock didn't work well.

"Need to tell the owner to do something about that stupid main lock. Sooner or later I'll break the key, and then he'll raise hell over it, putting the blame on me as usual. Wonder if it was even locked right last night," she mumbled while rattling impatiently at the door handle.

Heather didn't bother to write a note about it in the daily

report but simply punched a short message to the owner into her cell phone.

"Praise modern electronics," she said and got the admission tickets ready for the day.

Heather followed her usual routine, walking through the whole double story building, checking if everything was okay.

Employees needed to make sure all doors inside the museum were unlocked to grant tourists access during their tour.

All doors except the brothel chambers, of course. They remained locked the entire year.

Heather was sure she had to restock the gift store this morning. The weekend was just around the corner and as far as she remembered they had to refill some of the postcards. Surely a book or two was sold out as well but should still be some in stock in the storage room behind the bar.

As she walked downstairs the odd feeling that something was different that day made her nervous. Not that she would have been astonished if things had been moved around. Tourists had funny ideas from time to time, and Heather knew that weird incidents happened in the place during the night as well.

Not every night, but this was said to be a haunted building. When she arrived at the bottom of the stairs, she stared in shock at the open door of the first chamber.

"Now who in this god-forsaken town would dare to break open the locked door of a museum?" she swore.

"I don't believe it. How am I going to explain this to the big boss? By God, I hope nothing has been stolen. It would get me fired!"

Heather was furious, the break-in must have happened

during the evening shift. She had told the owner of the museum right away that the new girl was not the right one for the job. Heather had judged her as not very reliable right from the start and told him so.

"Weed smoking punk," she muttered. She hoped that nothing had been damaged in the historic prostitution chamber and hesitantly stepped through the door frame. At first, she didn't understand what she saw.

It took her a few seconds to realize what was wrong in that room. When the scene finally hit home, she screamed and could barely stop. Her terrified voice echoed from the cool adobe walls.

The McEntires drove to the Victorian house a few minutes before ten. They had come up with the idea to pamper Cheryl with one of Carmen's incredible breakfasts at the O.K. Café. The couple wanted to spend as much of the remaining time with their California friend as possible.

They both understood each other without words after so many years of marriage and knew how much they would miss Cheryl once her flight back to Los Angeles departed from Tucson. Both had grown fond of the young woman and wished she didn't have to leave.

When they parked their car in front of Crazy Anne's house, they heard the siren of the sheriff's car whining along Fremont Street followed by an ambulance only moments later.

"What's the commotion all about?" Bert wondered but Dorothea shrugged her shoulders. "Will probably not take too long before we hear it through the grapevine." She knocked at the door but Cheryl didn't open it.

Dorothea wondered if Cheryl was still asleep. After all, she hadn't been getting the rest she needed and the older woman was pretty sure that Cheryl must be exhausted.

After giving another knock at the door, the couple waited in vain for their friend to open. So Dorothea dialed Cheryl's mobile phone, trying to reach her.

"Maybe she's out, already walking through town on a last-minute hunt for souvenirs for her L.A. friends," Bert suggested.

The phone rang but no one answered. Just when she was about to disconnect the call, Bert's wife heard a phone ringing inside the house, probably Cheryl's. She looked at Bert. He started to knock at the front door again, harder this time. No answer.

Meanwhile a third car with sirens blaring raced along Freemont Street. A Tucson police car.

"What in the world?" Bert McEntire walked toward the street corner that met Allen Street and looked in the direction where the noise came from. His face showed a worried expression when he realized that they were all stopped in front of the famous historic theater. A crowd of locals had gathered already. The parked cars of the authorities had blue and red lights flashing.

"Something might be wrong with a tourist at the Bird Cage," he said to Dorothea as he walked back to the house where his wife still waited for Cheryl to open the front door. She looked at him, then at the phone in her hand, and all color drained from her worried face.

My God, the Bird Cage! Dorothea turned and took off at a rapid pace toward the old Adobe building up the street. Her husband called after her. "Hey woman, where are you going?"

But she didn't pay any attention to him. *I know where she is! Sweet Jesus, let me be wrong about this* she prayed while walking along the street as fast as she could.

Her husband followed but could barely keep up with her. By the time they passed Big Nose Kate's Saloon, they both ran along the boardwalk.

When they arrived at the historical structure, they saw Heather leaning against the shoulders of a policeman. She was sobbing.

The onlookers were trying their best to get the perfect view while pointing their cell phones toward the entrance. Everybody wanted to get the best shot of whatever was happening inside.

A paramedic wheeled a gurney into the museum. A hush went through the crowd. "Somebody must have been hurt in there," a lady in shorts and flip flops speculated.

Heather turned away from the paramedics. She saw the McEntire couple and reached out her hand.

"I am so sorry Dorothea. I don't know how this could happen."

The other woman stared at her. "What do you mean?"

Heather cried hysterically and nobody understood what she was saying until a single word turned Dorothea's blood to ice. "Cheryl!"

Bert tried to hold his wife but she slipped out of her jacket and ran into the museum frantically calling the name of her friend again and again. The sheriff tried to restrain her but despite her age she was fast like a cat.

She followed the noises coming from the downstairs area and crossed the main museum room as fast as her feet would carry her.

Downstairs, the voices come from the poker room, she thought. When she arrived in the basement the place seemed extremely crowded with people. Powerful spotlights almost blinded her.

When her eyes adjusted to the glaring lights, she realized the door to the first chamber of the fallen angels stood wide open.

Dorothea McEntire walked toward the door, yet hesitated. The gurney was in the adjoining room as the poker table area was too cramped to handle the medical equipment.

"Oh, God, no!" Cheryl's friend didn't want to walk any closer, fearing what may be ahead. She turned away but caught a glimpse of a shimmering green skirt, and froze.

"My dress, for the mercy of God, don't let it be Cheryl!" She stifled a cry as she set one foot in front of the other. The historic chamber pulled her closer, like a magnet. Finally, the frightened woman stood in the doorway.

The sheriff who had followed, wanted to pull her back but it was too late. She had seen what she wasn't supposed to witness.

Cheryl Roberts lay on the small antique bed. She wore Dorothea's gifted green dress. A few strands of hair covered part of her forehead and right cheek. Her face was the color of pale wax, and her lips were blue yet she looked incredibly beautiful. The lips had parted in a petite little smile. Her left arm hung besides the bed, limp. Her right hand clutched what looked like a large brown glass bottle. She almost looked like a Victorian doll from a time long forgotten and fit into the room unlike all the modern-day people who rather appeared as intruders.

One of the paramedics kneeled in front of her checking for vital signs. He slowly got up and shook his head.

"She's dead," he announced. "There's nothing we can do."

Dorothea broke down. How could that be? *How in the world did she get into the Bird Cage all by herself?*

"What do you mean she's dead? That's not possible!" the woman standing in the door frame yelled at the young man. "Try to revive her, for Christ's sake!"

He stared to the ground, not knowing what to say. Then he pointed at Cheryl.

"She must've been dead for at least 5 to 7 hours. There's no point trying to bring her back, you understand?"

No, Cheryl's friend did not understand any of this. How could this be? How could Cheryl be gone?

The sheriff pointed to the brown bottle.

"What is that? Let me see it."

The paramedic used a gloved hand to gently remove it from Cheryl's cold fingers that had turned stiff already. Fortunately, the glass was smooth enough to free it from her cramped cold hand. He looked at the bottle in disbelief.

"I'll be darned!"

"What is it?" the sheriff asked impatiently. The other fellow looked at the officer while he sniffed at the bottle. "The label says laudanum in handwriting! It's freaking laudanum, the stuff that knocked out many of the soiled doves in the old days. It looks like an original bottle to me. Where in the world did she get that from?"

Everybody was shocked except for Dorothea. She understood perfectly. Sobbing, she walked out of the room. When she met Bert at the entrance, he held her close. She cried hard and told him it was Cheryl down there, and that she was dead.

Bert couldn't believe his ears. How could that be? *We saw her only a few hours ago. This must be a mistake. It couldn't be Cheryl, or could it?*

His wife looked at him. "She went to be with him, Bert! It was the only way to return to Russian Bill. May God forgive us! We should have known better. How could we underestimate the power of the dark side of Tombstone's past? I'll never forgive myself."

Devastated, the couple left the scene. Meanwhile, the paramedics gently placed their friend Cheryl onto the gurney and covered her with a white sheet to protect her from tourists taking unwanted pictures.

Back in the Victorian home of Crazy Anne, Cheryl's open suitcase waited for flight AA 302 to Los Angeles. But Cheryl wasn't going back to that life.

CHAPTER 24

* * *

THE TUCSON POLICE CONDUCTED A THOROUGH INVESTIGATION OVER THE FOL-lowing days. Although it obviously was a suicide, her passing left a lot of unanswered questions. The police were determined to look into the case from every possible angle.

Dorothea and Bert tried their best to reach Cheryl's relatives in California. What in the world should they tell them? How could they explain the suicide of a fun-loving young woman?

The owner of the famous brothel and theater had to keep the place closed for the duration of the investigation. But not only that—he also had to provide access to every room including both bordello chambers, the small cellar at the end of the gambling area, and of course, the former bath and changing room of the gamblers in the basement.

The forensic people felt uneasy when the third door was unlocked. The officers hesitated to walk into the tiny room. Something was odd in there. When the door was opened after so many years, the air in it escaped with an angry hiss, or was it a voice? None of them were sure.

The sickening, sweet smell of decaying flesh escaped

the room as soon as the third door was pulled open. One of the forensics specialists had been working with the police department for many years, and he immediately recognized the smell. He prepared himself for the worst.

When he walked through the door, he stood frozen in the gloomy twilight. His face bore an expression of shock and disgust. The decaying corpse of a blond woman sat in an old-fashioned chair. A pile of silver coins lay on the ground next to her feet. She stared at him through empty eye sockets. Next to her lay the skeleton of another female on the dusty floor. A faded cape made of feathers partly covered her bones.

He tumbled backwards and hollered for the leading police officer who was upstairs. When Officer McCain arrived downstairs, the other man pointed to the third door unable to speak. No one had expected to find more dead women inside this building. But obviously they were not finished with unpleasant surprises.

The police turned the whole place upside down. The owner complained about the loss of business, but the lead detective made it clear that he would be lucky if the museum could stay open at all. The Tucson police department threatened to detain him if he didn't cooperate. The media was all over the place. After all, apparently it wasn't only a suicide that took place in the famous museum, but there was also evidence of murders now. The remains of three women were found in addition to the body of Cheryl Roberts.

The crime lab in Tucson issued the final report four days and a few nightshifts later. Two of the deaths were dated as occurring many years back. Not so the passing of the blond woman in chamber number three. The body was identified as that of Lisa Callaghan who had been reported missing weeks before.

According to the medical examiner, Lisa's cause of death was most likely heart failure. However, nobody knew how she had gotten into that third tiny room that had been locked for decades.

No explanation could be found for the coins lying on the ground around Lisa's body. Experts proved they were authentic 1881 Morgan Dollars minted of pure Tombstone silver prospected during the town's boom.

The female skeleton lying next to Lisa had belonged to a woman who had been around thirty years of age when she died. Only the skull of the fourth female victim was ever located, among the antique whiskey barrels and old furniture in the small underground cellar behind the iron bars. The skull had been there for well over a hundred years. Nobody could identify the two older skeletons but Dorothea assumed they were the two missing women she had come across in her research. It was impossible to obtain DNA evidence to be certain of their identity. Too many years had passed since their death. They remained unnamed lost souls, and the cause of their deaths would always be a mystery.

As for Cheryl, she had committed suicide by drinking the contents of an original bottle of the frontier pain drug known as laudanum. The weird part was that not a single bottle of laudanum had ever been displayed in the museum, unlike the bottles of embalming fluid, at the morgue, also saved from the 1880s. However, the toxicology report was consistent with the original formula from the late 1800s.

The night was dark and cloudy with no souls on the road. The main tourist season and the annual events were over. It was colder, and one of the rare Arizona rain showers turned some of the dust on the streets to mud.

The old brothel and gambling house lay in complete darkness. To the modern outside world, the windows were like the dark eyes of a stranger staring down on the street and peering at the opposite buildings.

But inside, the smoke was thick, and the laughter and music equally loud.

Can-can dancers tempted their audience, showing their legs beneath their swirling skirts imported all the way from Paris in the Old World. The dancers' costumes revealed more than would have been appropriate among the town's so-called pure women.

The poker booth sat empty next to the stairs. No one shuffled a deck of cards there tonight. Downstairs the longest poker game of all frontier towns went on uninterrupted. Some soiled doves provided whiskey refills to the gambling men, and some tried to lure the men into the cribs upstairs, away from their deck of cards.

But all that didn't matter to the two lovers behind the first door. A beautiful woman with dark hair and huge brown eyes looked up at her handsome man while she caressed his bare torso. She knew every inch of his soft skin.

Mae Davenport held Russian Bill as tight as she could, his moves throwing her into a frenzy of passion. She cried out his name as her female lust swept her away. Mae had followed her Bill through the gateway into the past for one and only reason—to feel his promised love and to find herself in his arms again like she once had over one hundred thirty-six years earlier.

***

Outside in the modern days, Tombstone was covered in complete darkness. The streetlights didn't reach the rear parking lot where Melissa always parked free of charge when coming to town to party.

"I drank too much of that dang tequila," Melissa mumbled,

her speech slurred, as she stumbled along the boardwalk.

She loved karaoke night at Doc Holliday's saloon, and the guy running the equipment was kind of cute, at least after a few shots. She giggled at that thought. It was obvious she was drunk.

She dropped her car keys trying to unlock it behind the Bird Cage and cussed like no decent woman would have ever done. She bent down, nearly losing her balance on her high heels but managed to get hold of her key ring. As she fumbled with the keys, she heard his voice.

"A silver dollar should be enough for you, little bird."

She turned but didn't see anybody. She shrugged her shoulders and tried to open the car door. Suddenly the voice was right next to her. Her heart pounded in her chest and she panicked.

If she had been able to see more clearly in the darkness, she might have made out the shadow of a man with glittering black eyes and the traces of bloody fingerprints on his cheek. But it was a night dark as coal, and no moon showed behind the rain clouds over the town. Nobody saw the figure of Mr. Hutchinson. An old weathered door opened in the adobe wall.

Not a single soul in town heard Melissa scream as he dragged her through that small door. Nobody witnessed her disappearance, and no one saw the door disappear after it closed. Melissa never returned home after that rainy, cold night.

But no one missed Melissa. She didn't have any family or a steady boyfriend. The man doing tequila shots with her certainly wasn't going to look for her again.

And the Bird Cage Theatre lives on, maintaining its reputation as the wildest honky-tonk throughout the frontier, as well as the most haunted.

RECOGNITIONS FROM THE AUTHOR

***

I DEDICATE THIS BOOK TO THE SOILED DOVES OF TOMBSTONE'S RED-LIGHT district and to the outstanding Bird Cage Theatre. The shady ladies and their customers, including the hard-working miners, played an important role during the heyday of Tombstone.

Without either group of daring pioneers, Tombstone would have never grown into a big silver boom town and would have never lured the Earp Brothers or Doc Holliday, along with other famous characters, into the settlement.

In the old days there were only very limited choices for women to earn a living after becoming a widow or being divorced. Sometimes they simply got thrown out of their house, or their husband "lost" his wife over a game of poker.

Laundry maid was one job possibility, but barely paid enough to make a living. It was extremely hard physical work. Sometimes, the only other choice was prostitution.

Women were often forced into the world's oldest trade, but there were also "calico queens" that chose the profession because of the high-income potential. Women were outnumbered in the frontier. Sometimes the ratio was fifty men to one woman.

However, the chances were quite high of catching disease such as syphilis or getting killed by a brutal lover.

Tombstone's town council earned a fortune on the shady ladies as each one had to pay a license fee in order to receive permission to perform her arts. One could say the soiled doves of Tombstone built up the town more than any cowboy or gunfighter did.

Many of the brothels were run by so-called madams who took 50% of the customer's fee. But often enough, brothels were also turned into hospitals when some sort of disease raged through a town. The "pure" women looked down on the women of ill repute. Strangely, their donated money earned in sin was accepted and appreciated nevertheless. For example, a large percentage of the contributions toward the building fund for The Church of Tombstone was money paid by the working girls of Sixth Street.

Tombstone hosted over one hundred ten saloons and fourteen gambling halls. It is said that over twelve hundred prostitutes "performed" in Tombstone during the mining heyday. An exact number has not been confirmed but records of hundreds of city licenses issued for prostitution provide an estimate.

The most astonishing fact may be that a license with the name of Josephine Marcus, issued by Wyatt Earp was found. It could be a forgery, but the lady was later better known under her husband's name, Josephine Marcus Earp. She tried to hide her shady past in Tombstone for the rest of her life.

The price of the girls' services per sexual favor varied from fifty cents to over twenty dollars in pure silver or in gold coins, which was outrageous those days. Race, beauty, and education, as well as cleverness, dictated the price a man had to pay.

The shady ladies mentioned in this book were real performers of their trade at the famous Bird Cage Theatre.

Mae Davenport

Mae came into town with a circus group like many other women of her kind. She decided to stay in Tombstone and performed at the Bird Cage as a soiled dove and entertainer. Only one picture of her was published, showing her in the 1880s version of striped hot pants and lace-up ballet shoes. She was a slim, pretty woman with dark curly hair. Her prostitution license can be seen in the Bird Cage Museum along with her picture.

She saved her money and later started her own bordello in the Mexican town of Cananea. Many Tombstone working girls joined her there, in Mae's employ.

Lizette "The Flying Nymph"

Lizette's last name and her origin are unknown. She earned her nickname from the act she performed at the Bird Cage Theatre, appearing to float across the stage and above the audience on extremely thin, nearly invisible steel wires attached to a belt under her costume. She made her trapeze act alluring to attract more customers into her bed. Originally, she came to Tombstone with the Monarch Carnival Company and, like so many, chose to remain.

Lizette soon developed depression and became an alcoholic. It is said that she died of an opium overdose. She was an exceptional beauty with long, curly hair the color of copper. Pictures of her exist in different books.

Crazy Anne

The character was inspired by Dutch Annie who was indeed a fallen angel of Tombstone's red-light district, but not only that. She was a successful madam running one of the houses of ill fame. She was the secret queen of the red-light district and friends with everyone. Dutch Annie was known as a smart, friendly, and beautiful woman.

When the outstanding, well-loved madam died, most of the population of Tombstone followed her coffin to Boot Hill where she is buried. Her real name remains a mystery. A picture of her can be seen in Ben E. Traywick's books "Hell's Belles" and "Behind the Red Lights."

Russian Bill

Russian Bill came to Arizona during the mid-1870s. He had long, curly dark-blond hair and kept an immaculate mustache, which added to his handsome looks. He also wore expensive clothing. He was quite well-liked among the females at the Bird Cage Theatre.

He claimed to be the son of a wealthy Russian countess and told people that he had served in the Czar's army but had to flee from there for attacking his superior officer. Due to his story, he earned the nickname Russian Bill, but his true name was William Tattenbaum, which is actually a German name.

He was well-educated and fluently spoke four languages. The Russian nobleman was able to carry on fine conversations about science, literature, or the arts, to name but a few topics. History has it that he was friends with Curly Bill, Johnny Ringo, and Ike Clanton during his time in Tombstone. He wanted to be an outlaw like them and joined in some cattle rustling action but was not taken seriously. He eventually left Tombstone and teamed up with an outlaw named Sandy King whom he met in Tombstone. They moved to Shakespeare, New Mexico. One day King shot at a storekeeper, injuring him severely. Russian Bill was not in town that day.

However, an angry mob seized both and hanged them. According to reports, Russian Bill begged for his life but nobody in town showed any mercy. King is said to have only begged for a glass of water, claiming his throat was dry and sore from talking so much in order to save his life. The bodies were left hanging for days as a warning for other outlaws that the town of Shakespeare did not accept rowdy behavior.

When the people of Tombstone heard about Russian Bill's demise, they were sorry to have lost the man whose manners and company they had enjoyed, along with his riches. Two years later, a gentleman appeared in Tombstone representing a Russian Countess named Telfrin, the name Russian Bill had given as his mother's. He sought William Tattenbaum, her long-lost son.

Word was soon sent back to Russia that the man had died of consumption because no one dared to tell the detective the truth about Russian Bill having been lynched by the locals in Shakespeare, New Mexico.

As for Russian Bill being at the Bird Cage, it is true that he rented his own poker booth for many months on a daily basis and had paid an outrageous amount in pure silver coins to the owner, whose name was indeed Hutchinson. His booth and gambling table can still be seen at the Bird Cage Theatre Museum.

Curly Bill Brocius

Not only was William "Curly Bill" Brocius a member of the gang of cowboys and cattle rustler but also a tax collector for Sheriff Johnny Behan in Tombstone. He had a mean temper, especially when drunk, and often used gunfire to get people to obey his crazy ideas, such as making a priest "dance" while giving a sermon.

On October 28th 1880, Brocius shot the well-liked Marshal Fred White in Tombstone. He claimed that his gun discharged accidently and feared he would be lynched. White testified that he thought it was an accident and that Brocius had not shot him on purpose. Curly Bill was exonerated. White died two days later.

There is no proof that Curly Bill was involved in the assassination of Morgan Earp. However, Wyatt Earp and his associates were convinced of his guilt. He ran into Curly Bill at Iron Springs on March 24th, 1882. Earp shot Brocius with buckshot to the stomach, almost cutting Curly Bill in half.

Nellie Cashman

Nellie was a pretty Irish girl who arrived in Tombstone shortly after the Earp brothers in 1880. She started a restaurant and boarding house called "The Russ House" and sold meals for fifty cents. She raised money for charity and the needy. Being a devout Catholic, she talked the owners of the Crystal Palace (including Wyatt Earp) into permitting services there every Sunday until the church was built. She helped sick miners and was the angel of the camp. Later on, she followed the gold rush to the Northern territories and raised the five children of her sister who had died of consumption. Nellie Cashman died in 1925 in British Columbia.

The Bird Cage Theatre

The famous entertainment building was indeed widely known throughout the West and even in some Eastern cities.

When Hutchinson the owner opened its doors at December 26, 1881, it started as a twenty-four hour, seven-day a week establishment that soon turned into a legend.

It is a fact that the soiled doves used it as their favorite playground. It served not only drinks but also other pleasures to the gents in fourteen booths or "cribs" overlooking the stage area. Two larger bordello chambers in the basement speak a clear language of the building's sinful past.

The longest poker game of frontier times was held in the very basement of the Bird Cage. Legend says it lasted more than eight years, five months, and three days, and was never interrupted. Legend has it that the wood floor could not be completed under the table as nobody wanted to interrupt the game for carpentry work.

Approximately one hundred forty bullet holes and documentation of twenty-six people being killed in the theater during its heyday give an impression of how rough the past of a mining boomtown had been. The theater and brothel closed in 1889.

The history of the building itself is amazing. Nowadays the Bird Cage is one of the most astonishing museums found in the Southwest. Many items on display give the visitor an insight into life and the hardships in Tombstone's past.

These days the Bird Cage offers spirit tours as well, and for good reason. Many have witnessed paranormal activities and were able to take pictures of it, especially around the funeral hearse.

Famous ghost-hunting TV productions have shot series of investigations at the theater and occasionally people witness orbs, weird lights, piano music, traces of perfumes and women laughing, transparent shadows, and much more.

The Bird Cage remains one of the most inspiring places to explore for me as a Western writer and even after countless visits I never grow tired of walking through it. It is a must see for me during each Tombstone trip.

The Black Moriah

The funeral hearse known as the "Black Moriah" had been the last ride for many of the people that had passed during the silver boom in town, according to local records. Its value as an artifact, as well as for the gold and silver trim, runs around two million dollars nowadays, according to the insurance of the Bird Cage owner's family.

TAKE A LOOK AT: THE UNFORGIVING DAUGHTER

* * *

CAN YOU ALWAYS TRUST THE MEN WHO RIDE BY YOUR SIDE?

Standing by the grave of her murdered father, Sheriff Townsend, Elli swears she will bring justice upon the killers. Unfortunately, the only man who can help her is about to be hung for a crime he did not commit.

Elli must free Armando Phillipe Diaz to defeat the outlaw pack led by the ruthless Texas Logan. A dangerous chase leads to a long-lost treasure and into a deadly trap. Will Elli Townsend survive and be able to fulfill her oath to her father?

"If you like your westerns sprinkled with gunplay, revenge, romance and unlikely allies; this is the book for you." – Rod Timanus

AVAILABLE NOW ON AMAZON

ABOUT THE AUTHOR

* * *

AS SOMEONE BORN AND RAISED IN GERMANY, AUTHOR MANUELA SCHNEIDER'S love of American Native and Western history might be surprising to some. But her fascination with pioneer life, cowboy heroes, and treacherous outlaws have been her constant companion for as long as she can remember.

As a child, Schneider recalls being mesmerized by American TV shows like Gun Smoke, Little House on the Prairie and Bonanza. In her adult years, Schneider fueled her deep interest in the American West by traveling to the U.S.A. and visiting historic sites like Tombstone, Monument Valley, and Kanab, UT. After experiencing the wild beauty of the Southwest first hand, her desire to write stories of love, struggle, and survival in the Wild, Wild West became even stronger.

After leaving a successful career designing motorcycle fashion for the European market, Schneider penned her first Western fiction novel in 2017.

When not researching or penning riveting stories about Western boomtowns and Native American life, Schneider can be found traveling all over the world, enjoying silver jewelry and spur smithing, studying archaeology as a hobby, and writing her own Western travel blog on manuelaschneider.com.